Silent Night

Other Folly Beach Mysteries by Bill Noel

Folly

The Pier

Washout

The Edge

The Marsh

Ghosts

Missing

Final Cut

First Light

Boneyard Beach

Silent Night

A Folly Beach Christmas Mystery

Bill Noel

Hydra
Publications

Printed in the United States of America

ISBN: 1942212429

ISBN-13: 978-1-942212-42-3

Cover design and photo by Bill Noel

Author photo by Susan Noel

Hydra Publications

Goshen, KY 40026

www.hydrapublications.com

Silent Night

CHAPTER 1

Silent Night, Holy Night! All is calm, all is bright, I sang as I took the early-morning, five-block walk from my house to the Lost Dog Cafe. Before you proclaim me certifiable because of my song selection, it's two weeks before Christmas and pitch dark. The cloudless, predawn sky was speckled with stars that went on forever, and for mid-December in South Carolina, the temperature was cool although not unbearable. Yes, all is calm, and I'm thankful.

The Lost Dog Cafe was a block off Center Street, the center of commerce and figurative center of the small, barrier island located in the shadows of Charleston. The Dog had been my favorite breakfast spot since I retired to the beach nearly a decade ago, and I was not alone in favoring the canine-centric, colorful restaurant. In season, the wait for tables could approach an hour, since it was not only the favorite breakfast locale for thousands of vacationers who arrived like swarms of locust, but also for locals who were hard-pressed to find a better alternative. The locusts, umm, vacationers, left as quickly as they had come and between Labor Day and spring, the island moved on laid-back, Folly time.

Two other things could be counted on during the

winter months in the restaurant: extended, daily visits by Jim Sloan, better known as Dude, and city council members Marc Salmon and Houston Bass. Today, Dude was seated at his usual table along the wall, but neither of the people with him answered to Houston or Marc.

He saw me and waved his ever-present copy of *Astronomy Magazine* in the air and pointed to the vacant seat beside him. I took his less-than-subtle hint and headed over. Dude could have been mistaken for folk singer Arlo Guthrie with his long, stringy, graying, sun-bleached hair. Complimenting his nineteen sixties look was one of his many tie-dyed T-shirts with a psychedelic peace symbol adorning the front.

Dude said, "Yo, Chrisster, Ho, ho, ho."

Dude owned Folly's largest surf shop, had been a resident since I don't know when, and was famous for mangling the simplest sentence. People who didn't know him well had sworn it would take a cryptographer to understand what he was saying. Those who knew him better had gone through a steep learning curve, or had access to a translator, but I had gotten the drift of his "unique verbal styling."

"Ho, ho, ho, back at you," I said, in the spirit in which it was divvied out.

Dude, at sixty-three, was three years younger than me, and at least three decades older than his tablemates.

"Chrisster, amigos be Finley and Teddye."

The *amigos* looked up from their eggs and gave me a bored grin.

I held out my hand to the female. "I'm Chris Landrum, and I assume you're Teddye."

It was a slight gamble on my part since their names could have been attached to either gender.

The attractive young woman nodded. Her long, blond hair contrasted with her black jeans, black turtleneck, and black boots. "Pleased," she said.

I paused waiting for more, but she must have learned verbal parsimony from Dude. I turned to the other stranger. "And you must be Finley."

He was also dressed in black, but his hair was bleached blond and as long as Teddye's. He shook my hand, shrugged, and said, "Duh."

"Chrisster, these be surfin' buds." He pointed to Teddye and Finley like I wouldn't know whom he was referring to. "We be jabbering about posers invadin', and skimpy, hot dog budget wallets they be haulin'."

Posers were non-surfers acting like they could surf and I guessed hot dog budgets translated as short on cash. Regardless, I had little to add to the conversation. I didn't have to when Dude said, "They be askin' Dude how to rid surf of posers."

I glanced at Dude's friends who stared at me like they would at a pile of pooch poop they'd stepped in. "What'd you suggest?" I asked to put the conversation back in Dude's court.

"Said be season of peace on Gaia—sharing, goody-good will, yada, yada, yada. Said to chill, let be."

"Gaia?"

Dude pointed to the floor. "Gaia, third planet from Sun."

Teddye leaned forward. "He means Peace on Earth." She rolled her eyes like she had to explain what a tree was to a forest ranger.

My phone rang as I was wondering how I could step out of this alternative universe, skip breakfast, and get out of the restaurant as fast as my aging legs could carry me.

I moved the phone away from my ear when it was assaulted by the ear-piercing voice of Burl Costello. "Brother Chris, my God. I'm glad I got you. Sorry for calling so early. Could you come to our crèche?"

Burl, more-formally known as Preacher Burl Ives Costello, started First Light, Folly's fourth and newest church, a couple of years ago. In good weather, its services were held on the beach near the Folly Pier, but when the weather didn't cooperate, which Burl said was the Devil interceding, services were conducted in a small storefront building on Center Street.

"When?"

"Now!"

I started to ask why, when he yelled, "Somebody stole Jesus!"

***

First Light's crèche, or Nativity scene, was located on a small grassy plot adjacent to Pewter Hardware and next to the Folly Beach Post Office. The slice of green space was owned by my friend Larry LaMond, a former cat burglar, current owner of the tiny hardware store, and for the last six years, husband to Cindy, Folly's police chief.

Preacher Burl referred to First Light's attendees as his flock instead of members, but either way, Larry and Cindy were neither. When the preacher realized it would be impractical for the crèche to be on the beach and there wasn't enough space on the sidewalk in front of the storefront location, Larry volunteered the plot of land. The spot wasn't perfect since it wasn't visible to most visitors to the island, but as Preacher Burl had pointed out, the setting for the event some two thousand years ago, which had inspired decades of Nativity scenes was far from visible or popular. He also had pointed out First Light's scene was within a short walk from Folly's three traditional churches, and using a little imagination, Mary, Joseph, Jesus, and the assorted bit players could see the houses of worship from the crèche.

The Nativity was fewer than two blocks from the restaurant, and I made the trip in a couple of minutes. I noticed what normally was festive Christmas red and blue colors flashing and reflecting off the Nativity's makeshift wooden barn and the hardware store. This morning, the colors weren't nearly as festive since they were coming from light bars on two Folly Beach patrol cars.

Preacher Burl was as easy to recognize as Dude. He was five-foot-five, shaped like a football, portly in polite terms, had a milk chocolate colored mustache, and a balding head inadequately covered by a sad-looking comb over. Today, his hair was even sadder. He appeared to have been awakened and had rushed to the scene without glancing in a mirror. The preacher was standing close to Chief LaMond and his arms flailed around like he was describing an attack by a flock of seagulls.

He saw me, stopped flailing, put his hand on Cindy's arm, and pointed in my direction. "Brother Chris, I am so pleased to see you. This is the darkest of morns for First Light. The Devil has reached up and with his evil talons, yanked our sacred symbol from yon manger. It's thrown our ministry into darkness." He pointed at the empty, rustic, wooden feeding trough.

Cindy turned and faced me. "He means someone stole the replica of Jesus."

Burl's conversations often slipped into preacher-speak.

I said, "Thanks, Chief LaMond."

Cindy nodded toward Burl. "I was telling the preacher it was most likely kids playing a prank and we'd find, umm, Jesus somewhere around town. I'll have my guys nose around for it."

Burl shook his head. "Who would steal Jesus?"

Cindy was a couple of inches shorter than the preacher, but better built. She pulled her shoulders back, ran a hand through her dark curly hair, and frowned. "Stealing the baby from nativities is so common, it has its own name: Baby Jesus Theft. Puts them at the top of Santa's naughty list, if you ask me."

Burl didn't appreciate the chief's humor. He

mumbled, "A sad day indeed."

Two officers had been photographing the manger and the other parts of the set, but I couldn't imagine them finding anything helpful. One of them came over and told the chief they had done all they could at the "scene of the crime." Cindy told him to tell everyone else to "scour the city" for the figurine. The chief asked if I could walk her to her vehicle and said she had something to tell me. I told Burl I'd be back and followed her to her unmarked GMC Yukon.

Cindy slipped behind the steering wheel and I leaned against the door. "Chris, for some reason the preacher is way too upset about someone absconding with a wooden statue. He tried to tell me why it was, in his words, priceless, but he was so upset I couldn't follow the story. He insisted on calling you—heck if I know why—I suppose he trusts you. He needs reassuring. This is not a big deal; happens everywhere manger scenes are. The youngin' will turn up."

"I'll do my best."

"Could you do me another favor?"

"Depends."

She put her hand on my arm. "I'm saying this as your good buddy. Could you for once, not get in the middle of police business; for once, keep your weird friends from nosing in our job?"

Since retiring to Folly after spending what seemed forever in a boring bureaucratic job with a huge healthcare company, I had been involved in several horrific events, including multiple murders. A few friends and I had stumbled, bumbled, and through tons of luck and a little skill, brought some bad guys to justice. Chief LaMond was more than familiar with the escapades and whether she would admit it or not had helped us with a few of them.

"I can't promise—"

She interrupted, "I know, I know, but please try. Remember, in the words of Haven Gillespie, *He knows when you are good or bad.*

"Who's Haven Gillespie?"

"Look it up."

My friend Charles Fowler had a habit of quoting U.S. Presidents and I had never looked any of them up to distinguish Charles's fact from fantasy, so I wasn't about to research Gillespie. "What brings you out this early anyway? Looks like your guys had things under control."

"Holy moly, Chris," Cindy said in her East Tennessee twang, "Somebody stole Jesus."

CHAPTER 2

Chief LaMond and her officers had departed—the officers to scour the city and Cindy to the office to wade through "Smoky Mountains-high piles of paperwork." I returned to Burl, who was pacing in front of the manger and shaking his head.

I put my arm around his shoulder. "Bad morning."

I was surprised to see him wipe a tear from the corner of his eye. What was so important about the replica of the Baby Jesus? I understood the importance of the Nativity, but Burl seemed more concerned than should be normal.

"Terrible." He shook his head. "Terrible."

I waited for him to elaborate. The temperature was mild, although the wind had increased and the wind chill made it feel colder. To get out of the breeze, I nudged him toward the open side of the three-sided, nine-foot wide, six-foot high, wooden barn.

He pointed to the figure of Mary. "Brother Chris, as you see, the figures are fiberglass. Through generous donations by those in our flock, we were able to buy them from a supply house I found on the Internet."

I wasn't a regular at First Light although I had attended several services. I motioned for him to continue.

"The structure was built from scrap wood donated by contractors and fashioned into a barn replica by me and others in the group. All this could easily be replaced."

Burl had been a carpenter before joining the ministry. "You did a great job."

For a moment, he didn't say anything and then he pointed to the crib. "Baby Jesus is another story. Do you know Brother Robert Daniel?"

"Don't believe so."

"You probably don't. Brother Robert had attended services a couple of times before falling ill to pancreatic cancer. After that, I took my ministry to his hospital bed. He is … was ninety-three years of age. He passed three weeks ago, two days after his birthday."

"I'm sorry."

Burl's shoulders slumped. "As am I. Brother Robert's son, Robert Jr. was in the military and sustained serious wounds in the Vietnam conflict. He was sent to a hospital in Germany to recuperate, and while there, was befriended by a local family, a family of quality woodworkers as only the Germans can be. Robert Jr.'s friend, whose name I can't remember, bequeathed upon him a hand-carved, painted replica of the Baby Jesus that had been handed down through three generations." Burl gave a slight smile. "Of course, it was not an exact replica since no one knows what the Christ Child looked like."

"Why did they give Robert Jr. something that had been in their family for so long?"

"I was never clear on the details of the political situation in their hamlet, but during World War II the family did not adhere to the radical views of Hitler, and when the Americans entered the community, our soldiers did not condemn the family and provided them with much-needed food and supplies. They told Robert Jr. they were forever indebted to the Americans, and the carved gift was a token of their appreciation."

"That's touching."

"Robert said his son tried to decline such a significant gift, but his German friend insisted."

"Was Robert Jr. with his father when he died?"

Burl stepped close to the manger and slowly rubbed his hands on the side of the wooden crib. "Robert Jr. had secured a position in finance when he returned from Germany. His dad said he was quite good at his trade and had earned a significant amount of money. He was to return to Germany to share additional thanks to his friend and his family for befriending him and honoring him with the statue. He planned to return the icon to its rightful owners."

"Planned to?"

"Robert Jr. was in a meeting on the forty-third floor of the South Tower of the World Trade Center on September 11, 2001." Burl bowed his head and whispered, "His remains have yet to be identified."

Once again, I put my arm around the preacher.

Burl said, "May I offer a prayer?"

He did, and we stood in silence. The wind whistled through the gaps in the walls. Typical morning life was beginning on Folly and a few cars passed in front of us.

"What do you want me to do?"

"Brother Chris, I know Chief LaMond and her officers will do what they can to find the priceless statue. They are good at their jobs. I am also wise enough to know a missing piece of carved wood can't take as much priority as crimes against people. It will be natural for them to lose sight of their quest for Jesus."

"You want me to find it?"

He nodded. "I have faith you will be able to achieve doing what others may find impossible. Your track record is such that it gives me confidence."

During my sixty-six years, I had been told by preachers I needed to find Jesus, but until this morning, two weeks before Christmas, never a wooden one.

"I'll do my best."

Burl smiled. "I know you will. And Brother Chris, I wish this not to be an undue burden, but Baby Jesus must be found in time for our Christmas Eve service. It must."

Holy infant so tender and mild. And gone.

CHAPTER 3

Burl had moved to the heated confines of his car, and I
continued to stare at the manger. Other than search the
backstreets and alleys and root through trash containers,
what could I do the police couldn't do to find the icon? There
was a good chance the chief was right about it being taken
as a prank and it would turn up. Burl had good intentions,
something he was never short on, but why place the burden
on me to find it?

I was wondering what to do next when I heard heavy
breathing behind me and a cane tapping pavement. The
familiar voice of my best friend Charles Fowler said, "Are
you delivering gold, frankincense, and myrrh? Couldn't
three wise men make the trip?"

Charles was a few years younger than me, had lived
on Folly thirty years, and for reasons no rational person
could explain, we had become friends. We were as similar
as a penguin was to a banana split, but there was no
explaining the mysteries of the universe. I had labored most
of my life in a bureaucratic office environment while Charles
treated work like it was a strain of malaria. I was shy and
reticent; Charles would talk to and befriend everyone he
came in contact with, along with their pets. He was a

voracious reader; I liked books as much as I liked ingrown toenails. Regardless, he would do anything for me, including risk his life. I knew because he had done it. I would do the same for him.

Charles was staring at me. He had his hands on his hips. His heavy, red jacket was zipped to his neck with the logo of the University of Alaska on its front. I started to explain why I was there and ask what myrrh was when he turned and pointed his ever-present cane at the manger and shouted, "Where's Jesus?"

"Gone."

"I may be old, not as old as you, thank God, and my eyesight's not what it used to be, but that fact didn't escape me. Did someone take him to change his swaddling clothes?"

I must also point out that Charles's sense of humor and approach to life has been considered a tad off center. Because of his disheveled appearance, unshaven face, and thinning hair that flowed to the beat of a different eclectic style, combined with his never failing to befriend the most downtrodden individual, others often assumed he wasn't among the, how shall I say it, intellectually elite. In reality, he was a textbook example of you can't judge a book by its cover. And speaking of books, he owned and claimed to have read, more books than are shelved in many small-town libraries.

"It was stolen."

Charles stared at the manger. "Burl will be heartbroken."

"He already is."

I explained about the preacher and the police already being here and that Cindy's guys had started canvassing the city for the statue.

Charles moved closer to the manger. He removed his Tilley hat and held it over his heart. "The statue's priceless. He must be devastated."

"Do you know its history?"

"Sure," he said, like who didn't. "He told me when I was helping build this." He waved his cane around the barn.

Charles had become a regular at the First Light services after Melinda Beale, his elderly aunt and last living relative, passed away. Before that, he had avoided churches for most of his life.

He appeared lost in thought, so I didn't say anything until he returned his hat to its rightful spot on his head. "He asked me to find it."

Charles grinned and waved his cane toward the center of town. "What are we waiting for?"

At some point in Charles's reality-challenged life, he'd decided he was a private detective. His total experience receiving a payroll check had consisted of landscaping and an assembly line job at a Ford plant in his native Michigan. Those jobs had ended during Ronald Reagan's presidency. Since then, he had picked up a few cash-only jobs helping restaurants clean during their busy season, provided a couple of extra hands for local contractors, and delivered on-island packages for the surf shop. He was also the unofficial executive sales manager for Landrum Gallery, a photo gallery I had opened, and after losing thousands of dollars a year, was closing. Regardless of plus or minus zero experience in the field of detecting, he had decided after watching countless whodunit television shows and reading more than countless detective novels, there was nothing he didn't know about his chosen field of work.

For the next five hours, Charles and I got a month's worth of exercise, walking each street within a mile of the manger. Most of our walk was east and west since we were limited on the south by the Atlantic Ocean and on the north by the Folly River and the marsh separating the island from the contiguous United States. The statue could have been taken off island, but there was little we could do about it. And, if Cindy was correct about it being a prank, Baby Jesus was probably on our seven-mile long, half-mile wide piece of land.

All that resulted from our efforts were four sore feet and two red faces from the increasingly brisk winter winds blowing off the ocean. We ended our search at Charles's small apartment, and I limped the remaining seven blocks to my cottage beside Bert's Market. I was exhausted, and it was only three-thirty. A nap was next on my agenda until I was interrupted by a knock on the door, and found two teen-agers on the porch, hands in their pockets, their coat collars pulled up around their necks.

"Good afternoon, Mr. Landrum," said the taller of the two. He was my height at five-foot-ten, sixteen years old, trim but muscular, and answered to Samuel Perkins. I had met the longhaired, young man my first week on Folly Beach. We had become reacquainted a year ago when he had come to me after he had seen a woman being abducted. Because he'd witnessed the crime, his life had been put in danger, but through luck and the help of friends, I was able to save him.

"Hi, Samuel. Hi, Jason." Even in their heavy James Island Charter High School jackets, they were shivering.

Jason Lewis was the other visitor. He was a couple of inches shorter than Samuel and wasn't as skinny and didn't appear as athletic. I had known Jason nearly as long as I had known Samuel, although for different reasons. I had dated Jason's mom, Amber, for a couple of years, until she broke off our dating after I had exposed Jason to a murder victim. Amber felt it was too dangerous for her son to be associated with me, but despite that, she and I had remained friends. Amber was also the best waitress the Lost Dog Café had ever had and was ground central when anyone wanted to know the latest rumors.

Jason said, "Hello, Mr. Landrum."

"Come in." I waved them toward the living room. "What brings you out?"

Jason looked at Samuel, who said, "Mr. Landrum, we heard stories in school today that somebody sort of took Jesus."

I nodded and wondered how the word was already around. "How did you hear it?"

Samuel turned to Jason, who looked at the floor, and said, "My friend Hector's mom texted him during lunch. He told us."

Samuel interrupted, "She told him some kids sort of took it."

I looked at Samuel and turned to Jason. "Do you know anything about it?"

"Us?" Jason inhaled. "No, Mr. Landrum. That's why we came to see you."

Jacob, Jason's father, had told me his son had a tendency to exaggerate. While it may have been true, during my talks with Jason a year ago, the young man had been honest and accurate in whatever he had said.

They kept looking down at the floor and failed to make eye contact with me. I offered them a drink to calm them down.

Each declined, and I said, "I'm confused, why did you come to see me?"

Samuel looked at me. "Mr. Landrum, we want to help find the kid, umm, the Jesus statue. If a teenager took it, he could sort of go to our school. Jason said maybe we should go to the police and offer to look around for them. I told him the cop'd say something like, 'Now son, we'll take care of it. You all go back to your studies.'" He rolled his eyes. "I knew how you caught the killer, you know, the one the cops didn't think was real. You were a stand-up adult, and are good at finding bad guys, so I told him we should come see you and sort of offer our help at school." He smiled. "Here we are."

I returned his smile and waved for them to follow me to the kitchen and pointed at the chairs. They sat, and I again offered them a drink. They unzipped their coats and were warming up; warming up enough to say a Pepsi would be nice. I was pleased with their decision since water, wine, beer, and Pepsi were the only choices.

"The first you learned about the missing statue was after Hector's mom texted?"

Samuel said, "That's sort of what we said." He turned to Jason for confirmation.

Jason nodded. "You don't think we did it?"

I shook my head. "Not for a second. I asked because if someone at school knew it before you said Hector did, that person might have known it before the police were called."

Samuel pointed a finger at me. "Oh, I get it. That person could've swiped it."

"Yes. What can you do to help?"

Jason and Samuel alternated telling me their plan which amounted to "sort of casually" talking to classmates and see if they knew anything, and to "snoop around" to see if anybody in the other grades had any information.

They were right about what the police would have told them, but I also didn't want them snooping. If one of their classmates took the statue or knows who did, Jason and Samuel could end up in danger.

"It's great you want to find the thief, and it could be helpful if you kept your eyes open. But guys, it could be more than a prank and if the person who took it finds out you're looking, you could get in trouble."

Jason leaned forward. "Oh no, Mr. Landrum, we'll be careful. All we'll do is keep our eyes open. Our history teacher says we need to be more, what's the word, Samuel?"

"Vigilant."

"Yeah, vigilant. He said good citizens need to do that in these dangerous times."

"Your teacher's wise. If that's all you do, it could help. The statue means a lot to many people, and it would be terrible if anything happened to it."

"I knew you'd know what we should do," Samuel said. "Vigilant, that'll be it."

I looked at each of them. "Promise me one thing. If you learn anything, call the police. If they don't take you seriously, call me. Think you can do it?"

Jason said. "Yes sir, Mr. Landrum."

Samuel nodded.

"And you won't confront the person who took it or try to get the statue back?"

They nodded.

CHAPTER 4

I grew up in Middle America where Christmas was wrapped in traditions galore. Mistletoe was prevalent in nearby oak trees, and dad made the most of it by taping pieces to each doorway, and a double dose over the door to my parents' bedroom. Mom took advantage of his strategic placing of the kiss motivator. We lived where stockings were actually hung from the chimney with care, although we didn't have a chimney, so our stockings were hung on a knickknack shelf over the television—with care.

Unlike most families, a fact I learned years later, Santa not only left presents under our tree, but he decorated the large, live fir that sat unadorned in the living room until the jolly one made his overnight visit. He earned the chocolate-chip cookies mom had baked for him. Santa had enough time to decorate the tree because he didn't wrap my presents, but staged them in their ready-to-play state for when I first laid my sleepy eyes on them.

It wasn't as often as I would like to remember, but a glance outside a few Christmas mornings revealed the ground covered with the white stuff depicted in many popular Christmas songs. Sleds had an immediate playground to slide across. Bicycles came with promises to be ridden once the snow melted. And, although there weren't any in our small, three-person family, little girls could begin playing with their dolls and easy-bake ovens as soon as the lights came on.

The birth of Jesus was never far from my parents' thoughts, although to my young eyes, Christmas was the tree, the presents, candy that was seldom available the rest of the year, and smiles of joy on mom and dad's face. We had a tabletop, ceramic Nativity and on Christmas Eve, dad read the Christmas story and mom tried to lead dad and me in singing hymns. Between my thoughts drifting to what might appear under the tree the next morning, and thinking our singing sounded more like a harmonizing trio made up of a screech owl, an alley cat, and a toad, the true meaning of Christmas was lost on me.

In the following years, Christmas ebbed and flowed in my thoughts. When I was living at home, I attended church with my parents. Santa stopped coming in the back door of our chimneyless house. Mistletoe appeared in fewer and fewer places, although dad and mom didn't need the seasonal incentive to kiss. For that we were thankful. The live trees that had enveloped much of the living room were replaced by a slim, artificial one which didn't need to be large, since underwear and socks didn't take up as much room under it as had bicycles and an electric train.

During the twenty years I was married to my high school sweetheart, Christmas was a time for a few days off work, a time for us to spend Christmas Eve with my parents and one cousin, and for visiting my wife's family Christmas day. We remained childless and never experienced the joy of helping Santa agonize over the *some assembly required* gifts that included instructions written in thirty-seven languages, none of which were English.

My wife and I attended Christmas Eve midnight service a few years but felt guilty because with the exception of funerals, those were the only times we stepped in a house of worship. After the divorce, I failed to see anything positive about church and organized religion. I was a spiritual person and believed in a higher power, but the trappings of the church did nothing for me. I expressed my need to help those who weren't as lucky as I by donating to organizations that helped feed, clothe, and bring hope to those without the means to survive. I spent several evenings each holiday season serving food to the needy, and being thankful I was fortunate enough to have a good job, and a safe, comfortable home.

Over the last year, I had spent numerous hours with Preacher Burl. Some of the time I thought he could be a killer and wondered how I would prove it. Thankfully—and in his words, thank God—he wasn't guilty. The rest of the time with him, I saw the hope, joy, and happiness he brought to his flock and most everyone else with whom he came in contact. He didn't smack people in the head with the Bible, but taught by example, combined with weekly lessons from the Good Book he translated into terms, which could be understood by all.

As he stood over the manger this morning, I had seen hurt in his eyes and defeat in his slumped shoulders. His hands had trembled as he caressed the side of the wooden crib, and his eyes watered for what was no longer there.

Was the theft of Baby Jesus simply the work of bored pranksters and the missing statue would turn up soon? And, if it was pranksters, they had little or no idea how the loss would affect others.

What if it was more? What if the statue not only had spiritual significance, but a significant amount of worldly worth, and was taken to be sold, or to go in the collection of someone who needed a valuable centerpiece for his or her Nativity? Or, was someone trying to make a negative statement about Christianity?

What could I do beyond what the police were doing to bring Baby Jesus home to be enjoyed as a symbol of all that is Christian?

I fell asleep wondering.

***

I awoke to a weather report indicating today's temperature would reach seventy, only four degrees shy of the record high set a century ago. It would be a good day to join the search for the statue, but before I headed out, I wondered if the police had already found it or if someone had turned it in. A call to the chief was in order.

She answered. "No, Chris. We haven't found it."

I hated caller ID.

"Why do you think that's what I wanted? Couldn't I be calling a good friend to see how her day was going?"

"No. First it's seven thirty, so my day hasn't been going long enough for me to know how it's going. Second, you're the second nosiest person I know, and it'd give you an ulcer if you had to wait longer to find out if the swaddling-clothed youngin's turned up."

"Guilty."

Cindy chuckled. "Shame I can't throw you in the hoosegow for that confession."

"Well?"

"Okay, okay. I repeat we haven't found it. Sorry."

"Hate to hear it. I know how much it means to Burl."

"I do too," Cindy said. "He told me each time he called last night. I had to tell him if we found it, I would come to his door, regardless of the time, and let him know. Then my wonderful hubby got on my case. Said the manger was on his store's property, so he felt responsible, and if I knew what was good for me, I'd better find the kid."

I told her I was going to look for the statue and asked if there was anywhere her officers hadn't had time to search. She reminded me the island covered more than a few zillion square miles of water surrounded by three square miles of land,

and that off-island the rest of the United States covered "more square miles than there were words to count them."

I thanked her for the geography lesson and with an overabundance of sarcasm she thanked me for pestering her.

"One question, Chris."

"Anything for you."

"If the little statue is so valuable, according to the preacher, priceless, why in "Blue Christmas" blazes did he leave it in the manger, in a deserted area, and guarded by a passel of plastic people and a herd of fake animals?"

"I wondered the same thing, Cindy, but seeing what condition Burl was in yesterday, I didn't ask."

Cindy said, "Hmm," and was gone.

The temperature may reach seventy, but it had a way to go, so I put on a light jacket and my Tilley to keep my balding head warm. I figured the police would have done a good job covering the downtown area, so I walked closer to the beach and headed away from town. I had made it a block when I saw Dude and his puppy skipping along the side of the road. Dude was skipping; his Australian terrier, Pluto, was running as fast as his little legs could carry him. Dude had told me a while back he had read that skipping had the health advantages of jogging, but at a slower pace. I didn't know where he had read it, although I doubted it was in *Astronomy Magazine*.

They pulled up beside me and I stooped to greet Pluto, named after the dwarf planet. He licked my hand, more in appreciation for me slowing his master rather than for being glad to see me.

Dude waited for me to finish my bonding moment with his dog, and said, "Surfer buds say you be cool for a geezer."

That surprised me since the number of words in my conversation with his young friends could be counted on two hands. "Really?"

"Yep, the Finleyster and Teddyetress be quick

deciders about peeps. Say you be okeydokey."

I couldn't think of much to say, so I limited it to, "Good to know." I also realized Dude wasn't as nosy as some of my friends so he might not know about the missing statue. "Did you hear about the missing Baby Jesus?"

He said he hadn't, so I told him what I knew.

"Terrible. Preacher man be devastated. Dude be riled."

He kicked the gravel, Pluto jumped, and I was surprised how angry my friend was. He had been involved in the problems with First Light earlier in the year, and had attended several services. He had told Burl he worshiped the sun god, but enjoyed Burl's services because they were outside and he could see the sun while hearing the words of wisdom from Burl. Of course Dude didn't use that many words, but I think it's what he'd meant.

I explained the police were looking and that was what I was heading out to do.

Dude continued to kick gravel. "Me tag along. Triple number of eyes lookin'. Me be pissed. Whoa. Is it okeydokey to say pissed about Baby Jesus?"

I said in this case it was and I'd be glad to have him along. Pluto wagged his tail in agreement.

I continued walking away from town, now with four additional eyes to help with the search. Dude didn't say anything—not much different from when he did say something—but I could tell he was troubled about the theft. Every other stride he kicked the sand along the side of the road.

Dude stopped, Pluto came to a more abrupt stop when Dude yanked the rhinestone-covered leash. Dude said, "Direction change 180."

I thought he meant to go back, so I turned.

Dude put up his hand, palm facing me. "Word direction."

"What?"

24

"Almost forgot. Boss crime wave on Folly." He looked at me.

"Meaning?"

He blinked a couple of times. "Vernon ordered two custom boards from *moi*. Shipped U Pee S to casa. Vernon excited and boogied to door for boards. Be gone. Boards gone, not door." He held out both arms. "Boss crime wave."

Charles wasn't around to translate. I guessed Dude had two surfboards shipped to a customer.

"Stolen?" I said.

"There minute." Dude snapped his fingers. "Gone next. Crime wave."

"Did the customer see who took them?"

"Negatory. Man in brown say dropped on porch. Vernon find empty porch."

"When?"

"Now minus eighteen hours. Day youngin' swiped from crib."

I couldn't imagine a connection, but asked, "Do you think the thefts are related?"

He looked down at Pluto like he expected him to answer. Pluto was more interested in sniffing a discarded drink cup. "Me be surfer. Think in waves. Folly small. Two humongous crimes same day. Boss crime wave."

I didn't think the theft of two surfboards would qualify as a humongous crime, but nodded. "Could be."

"See."

I didn't, but smiled as the image of a surfing Baby Jesus crossed my mind.

Dude said, "You be needin' to figure it out. Dude be pained to see preacher man sufferin'. He be helping everyone else. Now he needs help. Figure it out."

I started to say it's what the police were for, but Dude knew that. Besides, I agreed with him. Burl was a Godsend to Folly. If there was anything I could do to lessen his pain, I would.

CHAPTER 5

Groundhog Day must have come late this year. I opened the door to the same sight I had witnessed the same time yesterday. Jason and Samuel were staring at me with their hands in their coat pockets

"We meet again," I said.

Samuel smiled, and Jason said, "Good afternoon, Mr. Landrum." He looked past me into the living room. "Got more Pepsis?"

I motioned them to the kitchen, and they took the same seats they had occupied yesterday. I handed each a Pepsi and grabbed one for myself.

"Mr. Landrum," Samuel said, "since you're sort of in charge of our espionage—"

"Don't think it's espionage," Jason interrupted. "We're looking to see if anyone knows about the missing kid, umm, Jesus."

Samuel rolled his eyes. "Whatever. We're reporting in."

"Reporting in," Jason added, "and to see if you heard about the surfboard heist?"

Samuel said, "We think the baby theft and the surfboard one are connected."

26

I told them I was aware of the missing surfboards but didn't think it had anything to do with the statue.

Samuel shook his head. "Mighty big ass, umm, I mean, mighty big coincidence. Everyone who watches TV mysteries knows cops say there ain't no such thing as coincidence."

Jason shoved Samuel's arm. "Sure there is. Otherwise *coincidence* wouldn't be in the dictionary. Isn't that right, Mr. Landrum?"

I was amazed how quickly the conversation had headed downhill. "Yes Jason, there are coincidences, but the police look for connections before they write off two or more events as unrelated."

Jason turned to Samuel. "See."

Samuel repeated, "Whatever."

Time to get the train back on the track. "Anything to report?"

"Jason and I walked all over town after we left here yesterday. I know it wasn't right, but we sneaked through some yards." He tilted his head toward Jason. "He dug through those big dumpster things behind two restaurants." He paused and grinned. "He fell in one."

"I didn't fall in, Samuel. I caught myself."

"Didn't look like it. The point, Mr. Landrum, is we didn't find Jesus."

Jason said, "Tell him about school."

"Well, we sort of asked everyone we knew if they'd heard anything about the statue. We acted like we just heard about it and wanted to hear if they knew anything more than we did. Didn't want it to sound like we were interrogating them, if you know what I mean."

I cringed thinking about how the questioning may have sounded to their friends. "Don't suppose you learned anything?"

Jason looked at Samuel and then at me. "Not a thing, Mr. Landrum. Most of the students didn't know that the baby was gone."

It appeared the price of two Pepsis bought me nothing other than a discussion about coincidences.

Jason said, "Don't worry, we're not giving up. There are a few kids we didn't see today. We're still on the case."

I again cautioned them not to do anything that could put them in danger. Again, they said they wouldn't. I walked them to the door and wondered if they would know what danger was and how it could sneak up on them.

Samuel turned as they reached the porch. "One more thing, Mr. Landrum. About the coincidence stuff, I sort of feel like the boards being taken has something to do with the missing baby."

I smiled and told them to be careful. As they headed out, I wondered what the odds were on them following my advice.

***

I moved to the recliner in the living room and allowed my mind to wander back to some of my most memorable childhood Christmases, when another knock disturbed my sleigh ride down memory lane. Charles was standing on the porch, sporting his Tilley, wearing a jacket he bought in Gatlinburg when we'd been there a few years back, and pointing his cane toward the kitchen.

"Cooking supper?"

I laughed. The last time I'd cooked supper in my kitchen was—well, I'd never cooked supper there. Charles knew that, and I wrote off his comment as a joke rather than a symptom of early-onset Alzheimer's.

"Sorry, I was heading to the grocery to pick up some fresh fruit, vegetables, and tilapia, but got sidetracked by a total lack of desire and ability to cook it."

"So, are you coming with me to Rita's?"

I smiled and grabbed my jacket.

Rita's Seaside Grill was two blocks from the house and situated on a prime piece of real estate. The property had been the site of a bowling alley, and several restaurants before it morphed into Rita's a few years ago. It had one of Folly's nicest outdoor seating areas although that feature was seldom occupied in December. We chose a booth inside and along the window overlooking the Sand Dollar Social Club, Folly's iconic private bar, open to anyone with a dollar and who could wait a day to become a member.

Ashley, who had waited on me several times, was quick to the table. She pointed to me and said, "Cabernet," and to Charles and said, "Budweiser."

We nodded, and she headed to the bar. Charles threw his jacket on the seat beside him. He wore a long-sleeve, green University of North Dakota Hockey sweatshirt. I glanced at the shirt and looked out the window at two customized Harleys parked in front of the Sand Dollar. Charles had three more sweatshirts than a Dick's Sporting Goods store, and I had been trying for years not to ask about them. I had more to do with my time than to hear protracted stories about the schools represented, their mascots, student population, number of faculty members holding PhDs in Pan American Studies, and other trivia. Ignoring him didn't always prevent him from sharing.

He pointed to his chest. "Get it? Winter, hockey."

I stifled a whoop-de-doo. "Nice."

Ashley had returned with drinks before I heard more about the University of North Dakota than anyone outside Grand Forks would want to know. We ordered burgers.

Charles sipped his beer and glanced at me. "Has the APB on Baby Jesus captured him?"

An all-points bulletin was a slight exaggeration but said I didn't know.

"What did Cindy say?"

I shrugged. "Haven't talked to her lately."

Charles reached across the table, grabbed my phone,

punched in a number, and handed it to me.

"What did I tell you I'd do if I found Jesus?" Chief LaMond shouted.

I said, "Fall on your knees and pray for forgiveness."

"Not funny, you sacrilegious senior citizen."

"Couldn't resist."

"Ha, ha. Now back to what I told you. Didn't I say the first thing I'd do was call you if I found the statue? Even if the person who absconded with it was shooting at me or trying to hurl me off the end of the pier, I'll say, hang on a sec. I've got to call Chris."

"You did, chief." I sighed. "I'm here with Charles and—"

"No need to say more. Two nosies don't make a right."

"I suppose it means two concerned citizens asking the finest law-enforcement official on the island for an update on a criminal investigation."

Cindy giggled. "More like camel crap."

"You said it, not me. So, have you found it?"

She cleared her throat, Ashley set our burgers in front of us, the comforting smell filled the air, and Cindy said, "No, and it's not from lack of trying. Don't tell the mayor, but I added another patrol officer to the ones already on duty. They've checked everywhere. No Jesus." She sighed. "I know how much it means. Wish I could do more."

Despite a smartass gene she and I had in common, and her irreverent take on most things, Cindy was sensitive, sentimental, and concerned about how others were treated. She hid most of it, but the more I got to know her, the more I admired her.

"I know you do, Cindy."

"I wish we had more time to look, but things are heating up around here."

Charles leaned across the table to try to hear her side of the conversation. The nearby tables were vacant, so I tapped the speaker icon. No need for Charles to dip his hockey sweatshirt in his burger while bending over to hear.

I asked. "Heating up, how?"

"Damned porch pirates. Two more deliveries have been stolen."

Charles said, "Surfboards?"

There was a hesitation before the chief said, "Chris, your voice has changed."

Charles said, "It's not Chris, chief. It's the smart one."

"Oh, hi, William."

William Hansel was one of our friends who was a professor at the College of Charleston.

"Funny," Charles said. "Surfboards?"

"Nope. A woman's best friend."

Charles said, "Dogs?"

"No wonder you're both single. Diamonds, dummies. Yellow and white diamond pendant from Tiffany. Cost more than I take home in months. Snatched off the porch at one of the McMansions out West Ashley."

Charles said, "Wow."

Cindy said, "You can say that again—but don't. The other one was a bracelet from Saks Fifth Avenue. Cheap, only cost a thousand bucks. Grabbed off the porch of a house on East Arctic."

"Leads?" I asked.

"Nope. The homeowners looked for the packages within an hour after they were delivered. The thief must've been following the delivery truck. Big-ole brown trucks ain't hard to follow."

"A crime spree," I said, channeling Dude.

"Wouldn't go that far," the chief said. "It's part of the dark side of Christmas in the Internet world."

Charles tapped on the side of the phone. "From Jesus, to surfboards, to jewelry. Seems strange."

Cindy said, "The surfboards and the jewelry thefts

were the same MO. I don't see a connection to the statue snatch."

I looked at Charles staring at the phone and said, "The surfboards could be pawned along the coast, and the jewelry anywhere. Unless the thief already has a buyer, the statue would be harder to unload."

Cindy said, "That's why I don't think they're connected."

"It doesn't mean they ain't," Charles added.

"No, it doesn't. I wish we could do more, especially about the statue. A couple of my guys have volunteered to spend off-duty hours driving around in their own cars following UPS and FedEx trucks. They're also looking for the Baby Jesus. The folks who could afford the jewelry will have a decent holiday even without the baubles although I suspect they will spend a bunch of it arguing with insurance companies. Preacher Burl won't have a decent Christmas. I feel like crap about it."

I thanked her for the update and asked her to let us know if she learned anything.

"Not a second will pass." She hung up.

Charles stared at the silent phone, took a large drag on his Bud, and looked at me. "Okay, what's our plan?"

I was afraid I knew what he meant, "Plan for what?"

"You heard the chief. She said she wished she could do more to catch the spirit of Christmas thief. She was begging for our help. So what's our plan beyond walking around like we already did?"

"Begging?"

"Begging," Charles said. "Plan?"

"I've got to sleep on it. Let's talk tomorrow."

"It'll have to do. See you at the Dog. Is seven too late?"

I shook my head and headed home. I didn't think I'd sleep in heavenly peace.

CHAPTER 6

I was wrong. I got a good night's sleep and slipped out of bed at five-thirty, an hour earlier than usual. Rather than visions of sugarplums, Charles's question danced in my head. What could we do that the police weren't doing to find the statue? It was worrisome that it hadn't turned up. The longer it was missing, the greater the chance it wasn't a prank, and if it was taken for more sinister reasons, I thought about Jason and Samuel nosing around and about how slim the odds were that they would stumble across the thief. Slim still left the door open.

Was it possible the grab-and-go thefts were related to the missing statue? Cindy didn't think so. Other than stealing something, there were no similarities in the crimes. Again, a slim possibility beat no possibility. Regardless, I couldn't think of anything to do.

Charles had said seven o'clock, which meant he'd be at the Dog when the door opened at six-thirty. In his parallel universe, on time meant thirty minutes early, and he wouldn't let anyone forget he or she was late when arriving at the designated hour. I was not disappointed; I stepped in the near-empty restaurant at six thirty-five and spotted my friend at my favorite booth. He pulled up the sleeve of his burnt-orange, long-sleeve Virginia Tech sweatshirt and glanced at his wrist where normal people wore a watch. He didn't own one, but the meaning wasn't lost on me.

Before I had time to take off my jacket, he asked, "Got it figured out?"

I started to say no when Amber appeared at the table with my mug of coffee. She had worked at the Dog since I had arrived on Folly. The waitress was approaching her fiftieth birthday and was attractive with her long auburn hair tied in a ponytail, but her usual welcoming smile seemed strained as she set the coffee down.

She leaned close. "I need a word when you're alone."

I was confused. Not only did she appear angry, but also in the past she'd never hesitated to say whatever was on her mind in front of Charles.

I smiled. "Sure."

She gave a quick nod. "Want breakfast?"

In the hundreds of times she'd waited on me, she had never been this abrupt.

I said, "French toast."

She headed to the kitchen.

For years, she had been on a one-person crusade to get me to eat better, and would chide me for ordering my favorite artery-clogging breakfast.

Charles watched her go. "What've you done now?"

"I don't know."

Marc Salmon was the next person to enter and distracted Charles from questioning me further.

Charles said, "Yo, Marc, join us?"

Charles was not prone to ask anyone to join us unless he had an ulterior motive.

Marc looked around the near-empty room and sat next to Charles. "Suppose I can spare a moment until Houston gets here. City business never ceases, you know."

I didn't know that, but did know Marc's daily meeting with Houston centered more around gossip and sharing stories, some true, with his fellow council member than with city business.

Amber was quick with Marc's coffee but didn't make eye contact with me. He took a sip, looked at me, turned to Charles, and smiled. "Anything this elected official needs to know this morning? Always looking for ways to make your city better."

Anyone who knew Marc would have known it was his way of asking for gossip. Charles wasn't going to let Marc's agenda get in the way of his. "Marc, I know you have your finger on the pulse of the community," Charles said in his best suck-up voice, "Any word on the crime spree?"

Marc jerked his head toward Charles. "Crime spree?"

Charles seemed to forget about his quest for information and grinned knowing he may know something the inquisitive councilmember didn't. "You know, the theft of Baby Jesus, and the surfboards and jewelry heist."

Marc leaned back and sighed. "Oh, that." He sounded disappointed. "I wouldn't call it a spree. It's terrible about the things being taken off porches, and the theft of the infant was horrible."

I wouldn't call thousands of dollars' worth of jewelry *things being taken off porches*, but he wanted to minimize the impact. I did agree Baby Jesus being stolen was horrible.

Charles repeated, "Any word?" Nothing will keep him from his quest.

"I'm certain our Department of Public Safety is leaving no stone unturned."

"So, nothing?"

"Not yet." He shook his head. "I'm appalled anyone would desecrate the Nativity scene." He surprised me when he grinned. "I'm Jewish, but my kids love Christmas. After they were born, Mrs. B. insisted we put up a small tree. We have it to celebrate the season, but each year more and more presents appear under it."

Charles patted him on the shoulder, "Calvin

Coolidge said, 'Christmas is not a time nor a season, but a state of mind.'"

Add a worthless fount of presidential quotes to Charles's long-sleeve T-shirt and sweatshirt assemblage, his library-sized collection of books, and the handmade wooden cane he carried for no visible reason. If *Jeopardy!* limited questions to presidents' quotes, Charles would be a TV star. It doesn't, and he isn't, but he still managed to impress those around him.

Amber clunked my breakfast plate down on the table and left without speaking. Houston rushed in before Charles could share more words of wisdom from Calvin Coolidge.

Houston moved to the table where he and Marc often sat and waved to Marc, and said, "Sorry I'm late."

Marc told us he'd better join his friend and said to Houston. "That's okay."

Marc didn't share Charles's obsession with promptness.

Charles watched him go and said, "That was worthless."

"Not completely, now you know you can give him a Christmas present."

Charles watched me take my first bite and said, "Did you know Saint Francis of Assisi created the first Nativity scene in Greccio, Italy, in 1223. It was a live one."

I stared at him. "Should have told Marc, although he prefers more recent gossip."

"Going to, but he left. In a cave, if you can believe that."

"Marc?"

Charles gave an exasperated sigh. "The first Nativity."

"Interesting," I said, although I'd already forgotten where it had been.

"So what's our plan?" he asked, making a sharp turn in the conversation.

"Don't have one. Remember, the Department of Public Safety is leaving no stone unturned."

"Good, we won't have to look under rocks."

Charles said he had to make a delivery for the surf shop. Dude had Charles make local deliveries rather than using the more traditional shippers. Charles's deliveries were nearby and limited to small packages since his only moving vehicle was a Schwinn bicycle. I told him not to leave whatever he was delivering on the front porch. He said no way and excused himself.

Amber must have been watching because she was at the table before Charles was out of sight. She glared down at me. "Meet me outside in ten. I'll be on break." She moved across the room to clear a table.

She didn't seem interested in wishing me an early Merry Christmas. I'd better enjoy the rest of my coffee and the next nine minutes.

***

The Dog had two outdoor seating areas; one in front of the building and the other on the side closest to the city's combination library and community center. Amber was sitting at a table at the back of the side patio and out of view of customers entering the restaurant. The penetrating glare she'd used on me inside hadn't softened. She motioned for me to sit and made no effort to stand to greet me.

It was cold in the corner. I pulled my jacket tight and waited.

"Chris, what in the hell are you thinking?"

I didn't suppose she meant what I was thinking about what she wanted me out here for, so I waited.

"Have you forgotten why we stopped dating?"

I will never forget. It was because she felt my amateurish attempt to catch a killer had put Jason in danger. He had told me about loud television sounds coming from the apartment of someone I had wanted to talk to about a murder. The television was loud, but its owner didn't care. She was dead. Jason had sneaked in the room while I was checking on the noise and saw the gruesome sight. Right or wrong, Amber felt the need to protect her son from the events surrounding the body and put an end to our dating.

I looked at her and frowned. "I remember."

Her hands were balled into fists; her glare hardened. "Then what in all that's holy were you thinking by asking him to try to find the missing Baby Jesus? My God, the boy's sixteen."

Her level of anger shocked me. I reached out to put my hand over her fist. She yanked it back and stomped her foot on the wooden deck. "What?" she repeated.

I pulled my hand back and leaned closer. "Amber, I'm sorry, but I didn't ask Jason to do anything," I explained how Jason and Samuel had come to the house wanting to help find the statue; how they said they wanted to snoop around the school.

She flexed her hand. "Why did they go to you?"

"Samuel said it was because I had helped catch the guy he had seen abducting that woman. Said he could trust me."

"Did you insist they stop? To not get involved? To leave it to the cops?"

"I told them what they wanted to do could be dangerous; but to be honest, I doubt there was anything I could have said that would've stopped them. They're two headstrong, smart kids."

"You could've tried."

"Amber, I told them if they learned anything to tell the police and not to try anything to get the statue back. It's the best I could do seeing how determined they were."

She closed her eyes, shook her head, and whispered, "They respect you. They trust you. You could've stopped them."

She pushed up from the table and rushed inside. I remained seated and stared at her empty chair.

I thought about going inside and saying…saying what? I was sorry. But, sorry for what? Opening the door to the two teens, listening to their concerns. I knew they were determined to keep their eyes open and see if they learned anything about the statue and if they did, they said they'd contact the police. What was there to apologize for? Could I tell her I would have them stop whatever they were doing? I knew it wouldn't work. So what could I say? Nothing.

My phone rang as I continued running lose-lose options in my head.

"Dude here."

I sighed and grinned. "Chris here."

"Be having meeting at surf shop, sun duck behind marsh plus thirty."

I went out on a limb and decided since sunset was around five o'clock, he was having a meeting at thirty minutes past that time.

"Five thirty?"

"That's what me said."

Not exactly. "Meeting about what?"

"Surfer buds. Chrisster and Chuckster not be surfers, but invited—my place, my invite list."

Did I miss the purpose of the meeting somewhere in that? "What's it about?"

"Spirit of Christmas stealer. Be here?"

I figured all I would get from continuing this conversation would be a headache. "Yep," I said and hit end call.

CHAPTER 7

As anyone who knew Charles could have predicted, we arrived at the surf shop thirty minutes before the time Dude had almost said. We would have been earlier if Charles hadn't stopped me three times to ask what the meeting was about. I had thought the *spirit of Christmas stealer* had summed it up, but it wasn't detailed enough for my friend. He would have to wait.

The surf shop, written without upper-case letters for reasons known only to Dude, faced Center Street and was in the heart of Folly's six-block retail district. He had owned the shop for a quarter of a century and had stocked it with everything an aspiring or a lifelong surfer would need except for the ocean. To say it was cluttered would be like saying a few revelers gathered in Times Square on New Year's Eve. I was surprised after Charles and I had made it up the steps to see the space inside the front door void of its usual racks packed with wetsuits, enough surfboards to outfit half the island, and colorful swimwear.

Stephon, one of Dude's two full-time employees who were listed in Wikipedia under *Horrid Customer Service*, was shoving the last rack of wetsuits toward the back of the room while cussing the entire way. Dude was waving his arm and yelling, "There be go." I assumed he was telling Stephon where to park the display.

The shop owner saw us and turned from his employee and pointed to the space vacated by the displays. "Surf shop official meeting room."

I had never seen this much open space in the shop and it could hold a dozen people. Charles offered to help do whatever needed to be done. Dude said words that meant everything was taken care of. He added, "No be servin' munchies and champagne."

He had finished sharing the un-menu when three men and a woman arrived. They were less than half Dude's age and looked like a white rap group. Each wore black pants and dark gray hoodies.

The tallest member of the quartet looked around the open area. "Cool."

"I'm stoked, Dude," the second man said as he pushed the hood off his shaven head.

The woman pointed to the floor that had held a selection of surfboards. "Sick."

Charles leaned close and said, "Means good."

I nodded thanks.

The fourth person didn't say anything.

Dude waved them in. "Welcome to el meeting."

Charles, whose goal in life was to meet every human on earth, walked to the group and held out his hand. "I'm Charles, the boring looking guy over there is my bud Chris."

The newcomers looked at Charles's hand and glanced at me. The tall one who had spoken first shook the outstretched hand, and said, "Roscoe." He looked at the guy standing next to him who said, "Todd." The female stepped in front of Roscoe, shook Charles's hand and said, "Deb." The fourth person remained in the back of the group, and muttered, "Ryan." He didn't shake anyone's hand.

The door opened before I could say something like it was nice to meet them, and I had already forgotten their names. Two more people entered and gawked at the empty space. I recognized them from when they were having breakfast with Dude. Charles and I hadn't gotten the memo about tonight's dress code. The newest arrivals, like their predecessors, wore black jeans and gray hoodies. I thought their names were Teddye and Finley but waited until they introduced themselves to Charles in case I was wrong— something I often was when it came to names. They seemed to know the first group and nodded in their direction. Stephon had finished doing whatever he had been doing and joined the expanding assemblage.

"When're we starting?" Stephon groused. "I want to get out of here."

Dude shook his head. "Be waitin' on two more. Cool it. You be getting paid."

Stephon mumbled something I couldn't understand, and the door swung open.

Dude looked at the two men who were entering. "Me be psychic. Here they be."

The two looked at him like "What's he talking about?" A common response to much of what Dude says.

Dude didn't explain and pointed to the latest arrivers. "Mustache face be Truman. Skinny, youngin' be Slick Surfin' Sal."

I assumed it wasn't the name on his birth certificate, but the *youngin'* nodded, and one from the first group to arrive, mumbled, "We know."

Dude moved to the corner of the empty space and waved his arms toward the center of the room. "Gather."

The *official meeting room's* furniture must not have arrived, so we stood facing our host. The space was near capacity, and we stood closer than I was comfortable with.

Dude shook his head. "Surfin' buds Teddye and Finley wanted gatherin'. Said wanted to—never mind, Finley, be your meetin'."

Finley had been behind us. I turned and saw him look

at Teddye, shrug, and knifed his way through the group and moved beside Dude.

He held his arms to his side and then moved them behind his back. He clasped them in front of him like he was saying a prayer. Speaking to a group wasn't one of his regular activities.

Dude nudged him. "Words."

"Okay, umm, we all know some sorry ass thefted the statue of Jesus from the manger by the hardware store." He paused and most of us nodded. "We're surfers." He paused again and looked toward Charles and me. "Most of us. Where I grew up, Baby Jesus in the manger was sacred. Most times it was plastic, but to my folks and others in the town, it was the, what's the word, symbol, yeah, symbol, of Christ coming down here and saving our sorry-ass souls from evil."

Not quite how Preacher Burl would have put it, although accurate.

One of the first arrivers said, "Me too."

"Anyway," Finley continued, "we're surfers and often get a bad rap. Folks think we're bad and scuzzy. Me and Teddye decided we needed to do something. We can't have someone stealin' the spirit of Christmas from our island."

Teddye was standing behind me, and said, "Tell them the rest, Fin."

"Oh yeah, we heard someone had the nerve to steal two boards right off the front porch up the street. Now I'm not saying the boards are as important as little Jesus, but it takes a lowlife to steal them."

I wondered if Finley knew about the jewelry, but this wasn't the time to ask. There was mumbling from the group. I assumed they agreed with Finley.

Finley nodded. "Anyway, me and Teddye decided to organize a group and call it Surfers Against Spirit of Christmas Thieves." He turned and patted Dude on the arm. "We told Dude, and he thought it was a boss idea and offered this space for us to get together and invited the rest of you to come out tonight. That's it."

Slick Surfin' Sal, a name I could remember said, "It's horrible someone took the baby and the boards. What are we supposed to do about it?"

"Don't know," Finley said. "That's what we're here to talk about." He pointed at the group. "Ideas?"

The person who entered with Sal, the one with the mustache whose name I didn't remember said, "Other people may think it was, but do any of you know it was a surfer who stole the stuff?"

Finley looked at Dude and at mustache man. "No, Truman, we don't, but I was thinking since he," Finley glanced at Teddye, one of the two females in the room, "or she, stole two boards, it could be. Who else would want a surfboard?"

Stephon had been standing outside the group and leaning against a rack of T-shirts, said, "Someone wanting to hock them. Could've been one of the bums who hang around, or one of those hoity-toity guys who look down their designer-sunglasses-holding noses at us."

"Stephon's right," Finley said. "Could be anyone. What can we do?"

One of the first folks to arrive said, "Catch them and cut off their hands. Stealing Jesus. Cripes, it's as bad as it gets."

Dude stepped in front of Finley. "No to cuttin' off hands. Season of peace. Other ideas?"

"Hand for a hand," one of the others said.

Dude said, "Not be hand for a board."

Teddye said, "How about a reward?"

Dude gave an exaggerated nod. "Boss idea. Me be donatin' five C notes."

"Five hundred dollars," Charles whispered.

I told him I knew what C notes were.

Finley looked at Dude and said, "Let's pass a hat?"

Truman said, "Doubt many of us are carrying cash."

Dude smiled. "Me be puttin' hat on counter *manana*. Drop dough in."

Deb raised her hand, and Dude pointed at her. "I thought there are a lot of homeless people around here and others who don't have food. Dude, do you think we could take some of the money and give it to somebody who helps those people?"

Truman raised his hand. "That's a good idea. Lots of people slip through the cracks even with the organizations out there. Anything we can do would help."

Dude smiled. "Boss idea two. Bring big bucks and I'll figure where they can do good."

I was touched. I could be wrong, but it didn't appear there would have been many spare dollars among the group. I would contribute, although not five C notes.

Multiple discussions broke out, and Finley shrugged at Dude who raised his hands over his head and clapped. The talking stopped, and all eyes turned to Dude. "More ideas?"

The other female, Deb, I believe, said, "We could take turns and watch the Nativity scene from in the park across the street. Maybe the thief will come back to steal more of the stuff."

Finley said, "Good idea, Deb." He paused and pointed to each person in the room, except for Dude, Charles and me. "We could take, umm, let's see, three-hour shifts that'd cover all the time."

I thought it was a nice, generous offer, although from what Preacher Burl had said, only the Baby Jesus had significant value. I doubted the thief would return.

Dude said, "Cool. Sign up with Stephon for your shift."

Stephon rolled his eyes and muttered a profanity.

Finley said, "More suggestions?"

No one said anything and Finley thanked everyone for coming and suggested since the group was called Surfers

Against Spirit of Christmas Thieves the meeting should end with a prayer, and asked if anyone would like to offer one. No one did, and Dude said, "Lip-sealed prayer, be boss." The room remained silent until Stephon said to hurry and sign up because he was going home.

Charles and I stayed after the group had left and Stephon handed Dude the sign-up sheet that had the next forty-eight hours covered before mumbling another profanity and slamming the door on the way out.

Dude watched him go. "He not be playing wise man in Christmas pageant."

Charles and I agreed.

Dude shook his head. "Think meetin' be good?"

I told him I was impressed by how compassionate the group was and how seriously they had taken the thefts.

"Be good peeps," Dude said. "But they—thanks for comin'."

Charles said, "But they what?"

Dude looked at the floor. "They be fearin' surfer be guilty."

"What do you think?" I asked.

Dude looked up from the floor and at the door. "Want not to be."

CHAPTER 8

Like most kids, my early years were spent listening to my parents' music. Most of it was from a 1950s Magnavox record player where the sounds of Bing Crosby, Perry Como, and Frank Sinatra filled our modest home along with the smells of homemade spaghetti and chili. Being an only child, I had plenty of time to play by myself or listen to the music and my parents arguing who was the better singer: Frank or Perry. The rock-and-roll tsunami hit about the same time I was stretching my musical wings, and I fell hard for the rough, brash sounds that blared from seven-inch wide, thin, black, 45 rpm records; sounds dominated by Elvis Presley and Jerry Lee Lewis.

Then something happened. My friends were rocking along with Elvis, and I started enjoying the more mellow sounds of artists like Patsy Cline, Jim Reeves, and the piano of Floyd Cramer. Their songs were played on the rock-and-roll stations, so I didn't realize they were country. A year or two later, I would rather listen to Bill Anderson than to Dion; Roger Miller than to the Rolling Stones. I didn't want to be completely ostracized, so I did enjoy the Beach Boys and the Four Seasons, but country music either touched my feelings, my outlook, or simply sounded better.

When I learned someone on Folly was a country music singer and had charted a hit record, I made a point of getting to know him. True, his hit was pressed when I was fourteen, and the most fame he'd experienced since then was from several appearances on the Grand Ole Opry, all long before I was old enough to drive. Regardless, getting acquainted with Calvin Ballew, better known as Country Cal, had been a trip, and not only down memory lane.

Four years ago, through a chain of events that would be fodder for a country song, and a story that's way too long to tell here, Cal became the owner of a run-down, rock-and-roll bar a block off Center Street and renamed it Cal's Country Bar and Burgers. Little positive could be said about the burgers, but as a country music bar, Cal's had it all: an old Wurlitzer jukebox stocked with traditional country songs, an open-mic night catering to area-wide wannabees, and the "country legend," Cal Ballew, performing on weekends. To quench his patrons' thirst, Cal featured a wide-ranging selection of beers as long as they wanted Bud or Miller, and a wine selection that included everything from red to white, with vintages dating back twelve months.

Crowds, using the term loosely, were thin in the middle of the week in December. Tonight, they were anorexic. Of the six people there, I recognized all but one, a woman who appeared to be in her late fifties who was sitting at the bar. What Cal's lacked in customer count, it made up for in Christmas decorations. Three—yes three—artificial Christmas trees were situated around the room. Their multiple strands of colorful lights matched the strands Cal had placed on each non-moving vertical surface. More were hanging from the ceiling.

The six-foot-three, seventy-year-old owner stepped out from behind the bar and greeted me with "Merry Christmas." He looked like a living version of Hank Williams Sr. Cal's long, gray hair inched out from around a Stetson that had traveled with him for forty plus years and hundreds of thousands of miles around the South as he went from venue to venue singing his extensive list of traditional country tunes. In the spirit of Folly and the season, a strand of battery-operated LED lights was strung around the crown of his hat; he wore the rhinestone covered coat which had traveled as many miles as the Stetson; but, he had on bright red slacks and red tennis shoes. "Ho, ho, ho," came to mind as I gave him a holiday hug.

"I was getting us more drinks," Cal said and nodded to a table with one occupant. "Go on over. Wine?"

I succumbed to his high-pressure sales pitch and walked to the table occupied by Preacher Burl Ives Costello.

Burl stood and pointed to an empty chair. "Welcome."

Burl was the only person at the table so I pulled out the chair and now the *us* became Burl, Cal, and me. The preacher had told me before he'd moved to Folly he'd tended bar to make ends meet, so I wasn't surprised to see him in Cal's. Instead of beer, he had a can of Diet Coke in front of him. Cal returned and handed me red wine, my choice during the winter months, set another Coke in front of Burl, and flopped down in the chair. A slight mumbling from the other occupied table could be heard over the jukebox playing Skeeter Davis's "The End of the World."

I recognized the people at the table as employees of one of the town's small retail stores. From their colorful paper hats, I guessed it was their Christmas party.

I turned to Burl. "Heard anything about the missing statue?"

Burl shook his head. "No, Brother Chris. My heart is heavy and I feel such a tragic loss."

"The police are doing what they can. If it was taken as a cruel prank, it'll be found," I said.

Burl took a sip and set the can on the table. "Brother Chris, we are not going to be deterred. A kind, compassionate soul from the Methodist Church has offered the use of the Baby Jesus statue from his life-sized Nativity he displays in front of his home on Shadow Race Lane. He said it would be more visible in our setting and would tell whoever was overtaken by the Devil and absconded with our Jesus that good shall prevail."

Cal said, "Cool."

Burl looked at his drink. "Of course, his plastic statue is not as meaningful as the one taken, but I accepted his kind offer."

Eddy Arnold's version of "White Christmas" replaced "The End of the World."

Cal pointed to the jukebox. "My favorite Christmas song."

Burl said, "A pleasant one, to be sure."

"I have three versions on there: Eddy, Bing Crosby, and Loretta Lynn."

Each December, he added several Christmas songs to his musical selections. Believe it or not, he'd even added some recorded in the last two decades.

Burl was more interested in the statue than Cal's jukebox. "My heart is heavy about the theft, but my spirits have been bolstered. Several people who attend First Light have banded together and will be taking turns watching over the Nativity. And, in our common spiritual quest, members from the Baptist, Methodist, and the Catholic Church have volunteered to stand hand-in-hand with our flock overseeing the security of the Nativity." Burl smiled. "They will not be literally standing hand-in-hand, but will join our flock in watching over the manger and covering all hours of day and night. Praise the Lord."

"Burl," I said, "let me ask you something and I hope you don't take offense."

The preacher set his drink down. "You have my full attention and curiosity."

"I know how much the carved statue means to you, and was wondering why you left it unattended at the Nativity."

Burl looked at the jukebox, down in his drink, and at me. "Brother Chris, faith is the short answer. I had faith our fine residents would have cherished the icon as much as I did. I trusted the good in all of us would protect from anything untowardly from happening."

"Preacher," I interrupted, "you know—"

Burl raised his hand and stopped me. "No need to say it, Brother Chris, I once again misjudged the good in people."

"Preacher, it took only one misguided soul to take the statue. Your faith is admirable, and has served as an example for many of us."

I chose not to say it was naïve to believe the statue would have been safe where he had left it. I changed the subject and told Burl about the surfers and how they are keeping watch. If I hadn't, I could picture church members calling the police on the surfers, or the surfers trying to capture members of the Methodist Church, or combinations thereof. I also thought that while the plastic Baby Jesus would be safe, the hand-carved replica was still missing.

Cal leaned back and pushed his Stetson to the back of his head. I finished telling Burl about the surfers, and Cal said, "All will be well. I have faith." He turned to me. "Christmas, as Chris knows," he turned to Burl, "is my favorite time of year. All those years on the road, I spent most Christmas days in my car, eating the meager offerings from vending machines at the few service stations that were open, and looking around realizing there was no one to celebrate the holy day with. I heard stories from other men and women who were in the same sad fix—not only singers going from town to town, but homeless, or truck drivers, or folk between meaningful relationships."

"Sad, Brother Cal."

Cal shrugged. "It's what this is about." He pointed at each of the Christmas trees. "When the bar fell into my possession, the first thing I told myself, and all who would listen, was when the calendar page flipped to December 25, I was going to throw a—excuse my salty language Preacher—big-ass Christmas party and invite everyone who didn't have anywhere to spend the day."

"And he did," I added. "Country Cal's Christmas Celebration was a hit and it was packed."

Cal pulled his shoulders back and said, "Free food, free drinks, and free friendship. Nearly broke me. But it was damn—danged well worth it."

"That's wonderful, Brother Cal." Burl smiled. "I'm sure God was smiling over it."

Cal held up his beer. "Know what else I'm sure of, Preacher?"

Burl held up his Coke to toast Cal. "No sir, can't say I do."

"I'm sure this Christmas Day, if it's not too sacrilegious, you'll carry your priceless replica of the Baby Jesus in here, and I'll lead the group in singing whatever Christmas songs you request that'd best celebrate his birth. I promise."

I toasted the two, and prayed Cal's prophecy would come true.

The woman who had been seated at the bar had left, and the employees' Christmas party had broken up, and Cal twisted around in his chair and wished them a Merry Christmas as they left. Ned Miller was singing "From a Jack to a King," and we were the only three people left in Cal's when the door opened.

A man looked in the door and put one foot in like he was testing the water. He finally came in and closed the door. He was my height, had stringy, dark brown hair, a week-old beard, wore a faded army jacket, and gray dress slacks that were too large.

"Come in, Bernard," Cal said. "Come in."

"Where's everybody?" the man asked in a Southern drawl.

"Slow night," Cal said, stating the obvious. "Get you a beer?"

"Much obliged, sir," Bernard said, as Cal headed to the cooler.

Bernard stood in the middle of the room and looked around like he didn't know where to go when there were so many choices. Cal handed him a Budweiser and said, "Join us."

Bernard glanced at our table, over at the bar stools, and started to say something when Cal put his arm around him and ushered him our way.

Burl stood and reached out his hand to the stranger who looked like he would rather wrestle an alligator than join us. Burl introduced himself and pointed to me and told him who I was. I stood and shook Bernard's calloused hand.

"I'm Bernard M. Prine. Pleased to meet you, sir."

Cal pushed him in the vacant chair. Bernard sat, wiggled, and took a long draw of beer.

Cal gave Bernard a brief bio on Burl and me. He told us Bernard "lived around town" and stopped in occasionally for a drink.

Bernard waited for Cal to finish, and offered a weak smile, "It's warmer in here than out there." He pointed at the door.

It seemed clear Bernard was one of the growing legions of homeless in the Charleston area.

"Can be pretty cold," Burl said.

Bernard ran his fingers through his beard stubble, looked at Burl, and snapped his fingers. "Your church's manger had Jesus stole, didn't it?"

"I'm afraid so, Brother Bernard."

"Do the police know who took it?"

"I don't believe so."

Bernard was peeling the label off his beer bottle.

"Have you heard anything about it?" I asked.

Bernard's eyes darted from Burl to me. "Rumors."

"Rumors?" I said.

"Not that I believe them," Bernard said and glanced at Burl. "Heard it was a Devil worshipping cult, and one old drunk said it was a surfer." He shrugged. "That's it."

"Hear anything about someone stealing surfboards and packages off porches?" I asked.

Bernard gulped the last of his beer, and Cal asked if he wanted another before he could answer. Bernard nodded toward the bar, and Cal went to get another beer. The newcomer turned back to me. "No sir."

It seemed strange he knew about the statue theft but not the others. I told him what I knew, and Cal handed him his drink.

"News to me."

Cal waited to see if I was going to ask anything else, before he said, "Whatcha doing Christmas Day, Bernard."

Bernard coughed and laughed. "Let's see. Thought about flying to New York City and checking out the big Christmas tree, or maybe headin' to the Holy Land and seein' where the first manger was." He hesitated and held out his hands, palms up. "Instead, think I'll hang out around here and peek in windows at colorful trees and smiling kids. Why?"

Cal invited him to his Christmas celebration, Bernard gulped down his second beer, and Loretta Lynn sang "White Christmas."

"Might do that. I'll check my social calendar and see if I can work it in. Gotta be going."

"Beers are on me," Cal said.

Bernard reached in his pocket and pulled out a twenty-dollar bill and handed it to Cal. "Not this time, my friend. Got it covered."

Cal started to hand the money back, but Bernard waved his hand away and followed Cal to the cash register. I heard Cal say, "Win the lottery?" I couldn't hear Bernard's answer as Cal gave him change. Bernard waved our direction, and said "Merry Christmas" as he headed out.

Cal returned to the table, and Burl asked, "What's Brother Bernard's story?"

Cal stared at the door as it closed behind Bernard. "Funny, it's the first time he's had money. Sorry, Preacher. What's the question again?"

"What's his story?"

"A sad one. Bernard's been in this area going on a year. I don't know about before, but he's been in and out of homeless shelters. The boy's got a quick temper and manages to get in fights in the shelters. Gets kicked out and after so many fisticuffs, not let back in." Cal lowered his voice and shook his head. "He's one I call ghost homeless. I hear there's more than a hundred of them in the area. There're a handful over here. They can't stay in shelters; they, honest to God, have nowhere to go. They bum food, sleep in the parks or behind vacation rentals when no one's renting them. Damned sad—excuse me, preacher."

"No excuse needed, Brother Cal. I know of a few of the people to whom you refer. One's a regular at First Light. I'm taking up a collection in Sunday's service to give to them. I won't give the money to the well-known shelters or organizations that care for the homeless, but to a man in my flock who knows places where it can do the best for the unknowns." Burl shook his head. "I'm not naive enough to fail to understand some of the money will go straight to alcohol or things worse. I only pray some of it will touch these folks in a good way."

Cal touched Burl's arm. "It will, Preacher. It will."

Johnny Cash sang "Sunday Mornin' Comin' Down."

And Cal's front door flew open.

CHAPTER 9

Samuel took three steps in and slammed on the brakes like he was about to step on a rattlesnake. His hair stuck out from under a South Carolina Gamecocks ball cap. He glanced around the room and headed to our table.

"Mr. Landrum, Mr. Landrum, knew I'd find you here," he said and stopped and looked at Burl and Cal.

"How'd you know?"

He removed his cap and held it to his side. Static electricity wreaked havoc with his hair. "Everybody sort of knows this is where you hang out."

I needed to work on my image. I was here with a preacher, so that should count for something.

Cal said, "Getcha a Coke or bottle of water?"

"Umm, no, thank you, Mr. Cal. I'm okay."

"What can I do for you?" I asked. I watched as Samuel squeezed his cap and pushed his hair out of his face with the other hand.

"Could we talk to you?"

"We?"

"Jason and I."

"Where's Jason?"

Samuel looked down at the foot-worn thin, beer-stained carpet. "He's outside. He said his mom would sort of kill him if she found out he was in a bar. Could you come out and talk to us?"

I was in enough trouble with Amber and didn't want to incur more grief if she learned I was meeting with her son in Cal's sin-den. "Sure."

I grabbed my coat and followed the teen.

"Merry Christmas, Brother Samuel," Burl hollered as we walked away.

Samuel turned and smiled. "Thank you, Preacher Burl, sir."

Samuel led me a half-block up the street to the boys' bikes. Jason was sitting on his, and his eyes darted around like he was selling dope and hoped the police wouldn't see him. It was windy and cold, and he had his dark green, quilted jacket zipped to his neck. He wore gloves and a navy and gold Charleston RiverDogs cap.

"Thank goodness Samuel found you. We went to your house, and your car was there, but you didn't answer."

"What's going on?"

Samuel moved beside Jason and looked at him. "You tell him."

"I thought you," Jason said. "Never mind. Mr. Landrum, Samuel and I were riding by the Nativity a half hour ago and—"

Samuel interrupted. "Sort of like an hour ago."

"Okay," Jason said. "We were riding by, and Samuel saw a person—"

Samuel interrupted—again. "Suspicious character."

Jason jerked his head toward Samuel. "You going to tell it?"

"Sorry, go on."

Jason continued, "Anyway, the person, the suspicious character, was in the barn-like thing, and Samuel said he looked like he was going to steal something. We rode on by like we didn't see anything and parked our bikes and sneaked back to the barn."

"We weren't going to try to catch him, Mr. Landrum," Samuel added. "Honest. All we wanted to do was take his picture with the camera on my phone and tell the police."

"Humph," Jason interrupted. "Right when we were beside the barn, the person must have seen us. He took out running that way on Indian Avenue." He waved his hand toward the east. "We didn't get the picture so we started running after him."

Samuel said, "He had a big head start, Mr. Landrum. Our bikes were the other direction so we didn't have time to get them and ride after him. He was pretty swift but we were catching up."

"Until Samuel fell in a hole."

I glanced down and saw mud caked on Samuel's knee. "You okay?"

"Sure, nothing bad." Samuel looked at Jason. "Don't forget to tell him about what the stop sign did."

Jason gave Samuel a dirty look. "Bigmouth. Well, Mr. Landrum, after Samuel got up we started running again. It's mighty dark out there. I, umm, ran into a stop sign. Didn't see it."

Samuel laughed. "It honest to God meant stop."

"Are you okay?" I was beginning to sound like their mother.

Jason took off his cap, and I saw the red mark on his forehead. "Just a bruise. Mom'll kill me if she finds out."

"Then what happened?"

Samuel looked at Jason and said, "Sort of nothing."

"By the time we stopped and started twice, the thief was gone. It was dark."

"Did you get a good look at him?"

Samuel shrugged. "No. Don't even know if it was a guy."

"If it was a lady," Jason said, "she was tall, maybe as

tall as Samuel. He, or she, had on an overcoat kind of coat."

"And one of those stretchy hats that pulls over the ears," Samuel said.

"Anything else?" I asked.

"Fast," Jason said.

Samuel looked off into space like he was trying to picture the person. "And old, maybe even forty."

I considered giving Samuel another bruise.

Jason said, "That's about it, Mr. Landrum."

"What made you think the person was going to steal something rather than looking at the Nativity? Could he have come from looking at the city's Christmas light display in the park across the street?"

Samuel looked at Jason, and at me. "He sort of looked sneaky. Didn't look like he was admiring the stuff, he wanted to steal it."

"But you only got a glance when you rode by?"

Samuel said, "Yeah."

"Could you have thought he looked suspicious because someone had taken the statue and you thought the person would return to steal something else?"

"Umm, maybe," Jason said.

"And you were just riding by the Nativity?"

"Sort of," Samuel said.

Jason nodded.

And they expect me to believe that, I thought. I remembered what the surfers had said during their meeting. "Did you see anyone else?"

"Yeah," Samuel said. "The first, or maybe it was the second, time we rode by there was one of those surfer dudes sleeping in the park across the street. He was curled up in a sleeping bag on the side of the path with the bright Christmas displays, so we didn't figure he was going to steal anything."

So much for the surfers' twenty-four-seven security.

"And that's it?"

"Yeah," Samuel said.

Jason said, "Yes sir."

Other than learning someone was looking at the Nativity, and he, or she, ran when two teenagers started chasing, a reaction that didn't seem abnormal considering the circumstances; and, learning the surfer patrol appeared less than effective; and, learning my two young friends were more clumsy than I would have thought; I hadn't heard anything to tie what happened to the theft of the statue, the surfboards, or the jewelry. Oh yeah, I was reminded Jason and Samuel had overactive imaginations.

Jason rubbed his shoe in the sand beside the sidewalk. "Mr. Landrum, you're not going to tell mom about this are you?"

I gave him a stern look. "Not this time. But listen, you said you were just riding by the Nativity, yet you told me you rode by two or maybe three times. Looks like you were riding by and hoping to catch the thief. Is that close?"

Samuel mumbled, "Sort of." Jason didn't say anything.

"That's what I thought. Now, what if the person you saw was the thief. He could have pulled a gun instead of running. Then what would have happened?"

Samuel took a step back. "Didn't think of that."

A typical teenager's response: *I'm indestructible.*

"I want both of you to go home and spend time thinking about what might have happened. I know you want the thief caught. I admire you for that. I want it too, and so do the police. They're doing everything possible to find the statue." I stared at Jason and at Samuel. "Leave it to them."

Jason hung his head, and Samuel stared at my feet. Jason whispered, "Yes sir."

"Good," I said and pulled them close and gave them a hug. "Thanks for coming to tell me. Now get home."

CHAPTER 10

I woke up hungry and started to go to the Dog for a hearty breakfast, but the more I thought about last night and the potential danger Amber's son and his friend could have gotten into, I wasn't ready to face her. If Jason had told his mom what he had done yesterday and let it slip he came to talk to me, she'd meet me at the door with a rolling pin, if those things still existed, rather than with her warm smile. I wasn't ready for that fate this cold, crisp December morning.

I searched my kitchen, a task that couldn't have taken more than thirty seconds, since my food supply would be hard-pressed to feed a family of four—mice. Hidden behind an empty cereal box I had saved for unknown reasons, I found a muffin I had bought at Bert's a week ago. It wasn't quite hard enough to pound a nail through hardwood, so I stuck it in the microwave and softened it enough so it wouldn't shatter my teeth.

It tasted better than eating the cereal box and gave me enough energy to sit and worry about what Jason and Samuel were doing. They were well intended, although had no idea what they were dealing with. None of us did. Was the statue taken as a prank by someone harmless who will abandon it and get a laugh out of it? Did someone who made a habit of stealing take it; someone, if confronted, might resort to violence rather than being caught? Considering how valuable Burl had said the icon was, could it have been taken by someone who realized its value and planned to sell it to a collector; someone who if confronted would stop at nothing to get away with it? Was the person Jason and Samuel chased running because he, or she, planned to steal something or simply was startled by two teens wearing dark clothes?

I took the last bite, stared at the empty paper plate, and wondered if there was a connection between the theft of the icon, the surfboards, and the jewelry. All I realized after finishing the muffin and asking myself several questions was that I didn't have answers, but had a kitchen devoid of anything edible.

Most of my grocery shopping was restricted to Bert's Market, my iconic next-door neighbor, but I made at least one trip to the nearest big-box grocery every six months, whether I needed to or not. I spent the next hour driving off-island, stumbling dazed-and-confused through the aisles of Harris Teeter while pretending like I knew what I was doing. Christmas was around the corner, so I felt obligated to buy two boxes of Christmas cookies; holiday fruitcakes had a shelf life of three hundred years, so I grabbed one, and I selected a colorful box of Cheez-It crackers. I was more at home when I reached the wine department, and selected three bottles of the finest, screw top Cabernets. I headed to the checkout line feeling like a true grocery shopper.

On the drive home, I swung by the Nativity. Everything looked like it should and the borrowed Baby Jesus fit with the rest of the pieces. I didn't notice surfers or church members guarding the display but didn't stop to check. I was sure someone was nearby, and maybe awake. I pulled in the drive and was unloading grocery bags when I saw Jason and Samuel peddling up the street. My cottage faced one of Folly's busiest roads, and I hoped the teens realized bikes versus cars wouldn't be a fair match. I noticed a UPS truck a block ahead of my young friends. The truck turned left two blocks up, and Jason and Samuel did the same.

Oh great. I may as well have been lecturing to their bikes last night. I threw the bags back in the car and followed the mini-parade. The brown delivery truck had stopped in the street ahead of me, but I lost sight of Jason and Samuel. I was wondering where they were when Jason's head peeked over a shrub row a half block behind the truck.

The driver returned to his truck and moved on. I pulled off the side of the road ten feet behind the bicycles. Samuel was getting back on his when he heard me opening the car door. He jumped, and his bike clanked to the driveway where it had been hidden.

He grabbed his chest. "Geez, Mr. Landrum, you scared the shi—umm, crap out of me."

Jason was beside Samuel and chuckled at Samuel's reaction. "Didn't scare me. I knew it was you."

Samuel righted his bike and glared at Jason.

I slammed the door and stared at the boys. "What do you think you're doing?"

Samuel leaned against his handlebars and glanced at Jason. "Mr. Landrum, we're just out for a ride. The weather's not cold, and we're out of school. Peddling's good exercise, you know."

I pointed my thumb over my shoulder in the direction the UPS truck had gone. "And your ride had nothing to do with that truck?"

Samuel looked toward where I had been pointing. "Well—"

Jason interrupted, "It did."

Samuel said, "We were sort of following it."

"To catch the person who's stealing packages," I added and shook my head. "And what were you going to do if you saw him?"

Each boy reached for his phone.

Jason said, "We were going to take his picture and call the cops."

"That's all?"

Jason said, "Yes sir."

"When I pulled up, did you know who it was?"

Jason nodded; Samuel shook his head.

"What if it was the thief? You might think you were sneaky, but you were about as conspicuous as two Hershey Kisses in a pile of M&Ms." They both looked at their feet. "I'm serious fellas. Leave it to the police."

They mumbled, groused, stood with slumped shoulders, and said they understood. I'm sure they meant it—for the moment.

***

Charles stopped by the house mid-afternoon. He threw his jacket on the table by the door and his Tilley on top of it. He wore heavy corduroy slacks and a blue, long-sleeve Widener University sweatshirt with a gold lion's head on the front.

"I've been thinking," he said.

Always dangerous, I thought. I motioned for him to continue.

"Surfboards, diamonds and gold, all things that could be sold."

I hoped that wasn't the result of his thinking. "So?"

"Cindy tells us every year thefts increase around Christmas. Munchkin mouths to feed, gifts to buy, other stuff. Stealing the boards and the jewelry makes sense." He stared at me like I was supposed to say something profound. I didn't, so he continued, "But what's with stealing Jesus? I know it's valuable, but isn't most of the value sentimental? The other things could easily be pawned, except what pawn shop would give more than a few dollars for a wooden statue, even if it's Jesus?"

"Charles, we don't know the thefts are related."

"So true, oh wise one. Let's say they aren't, although I think they are. And, let's say whoever stole Jesus isn't building a hand-carved Nativity and needed a baby to stick in it and instead wants to turn the Christ Child into cash. Where would he be able to sell it for near what it's worth?"

Since Charles had been thinking about it, I figured I'd better give him the first crack at an answer. "Where?"

He shrugged. "Heck if I know."

I wondered how much thought he'd given to come up with that.

"There's still a chance it was a prank," I said.

"Don't that seem less likely every day that goes by?"

"True."

"Yep, it's what Cindy said this morning in the Dog. Said she's about given up on finding Jesus hanging around on the streets or lounging by the pool at the Tides Hotel. Dude was there and said if it was still around, his surfer group would find it. To tell the truth, he didn't seem more hopeful than the chief." Charles looked at the ceiling and out the window. "So back to my first question, where could the spirit of Christmas thief sell it?"

"Not a pawn shop," I said.

Charles nodded.

"This was the first year for Burl's Nativity scene so no one knew about the statue from other years and planned to take it this season. If it wasn't spontaneous, it couldn't have been planned long. The thief probably wouldn't have taken it unless he knew there was a good chance he had a buyer."

"What's that tell us?" Charles asked.

"Not much, just trying to talk it through."

"John Kennedy said, 'You know nothing for sure except the fact that you know nothing for sure.'"

I rolled my eyes.

Charles shrugged, "Thought it fit." He rubbed his five-day-old beard. "Anyway, the statue was old."

"According to Burl, a hundred years old and could have been more."

"From Germany," Charles added.

"Antique dealer?"

Charles said, "Could be."

"A crooked one."

"Why crooked?" Charles asked. "Don't antique dealers buy old stuff?"

"Yes, but there's been one newspaper story about the theft, and it was on television and radio. No reputable dealer'd touch it."

"So all we have to do is find the crooked antique dealer, beat him in the head with thy rod and thy staff until he coughs up Baby Jesus."

"And how do you plan to do that?"

"Don't suppose any of the antique dealers' yellow page ads say anything about specializing in stolen Baby Jesus statues?"

It didn't deserve a response, and I was ready to suggest we talk to Chief LaMond, when the phone rang.

A high-pitched voice said, "Is this Chris Landrum?"

"Yes."

"This is Finley. You may not remember, but I met you in the Dog when I was with Dude. I also saw you at the surfers' meeting at the surf shop."

In fact, I did remember, mainly from the Dog. "Sure, I remember."

"Oh." He seemed surprised. "Well, I got your number from Dude. We're having a meeting tonight and wanted you to come."

"Who's meeting?"

"The group from the surf shop."

"Meeting where?"

"My house."

I said, "Why me?"

"Dude told me how good you were at catching bad

guys and told me to invite you. We want to catch whoever's giving us a bad rap by stealing boards, and we're bummed about the statue. Could you come?"

I told him yes. He gave me directions and time, and I asked if Charles could come. He said, "Whatever."

I told Charles about the meeting.

"Now we're getting somewhere."

We were?

CHAPTER 11

Finley's house was on East Erie Avenue near 3rd Street, and four blocks from the ocean. The large, two-story, elevated structure's wood siding was black from weather and age with a second-floor balcony that spanned the front. A wide set of stairs led to the front door, and there was a newer set of stairs on the side of the house that led to the top floor. A tarp-covered vehicle and two motorcycles were parked under the house along with two sawhorses supporting sheets of plywood, and a Datsun pick-up truck missing its front two wheels was beside the house. Two cars were parked in the front yard, and another vehicle was off the side of the road with a newer model Ford pickup parked behind it with *Landscaping R Us* stenciled on the door. Two of the cars had surfboard racks. The house on each side of Finley's had fading *For Rent* signs in the front yards, while the houses across the street were newer and one was well landscaped and maintained, and probably occupied by permanent residents.

Rock music blared from the house, and the faint smell of marijuana greeted us at the door. Finley, wearing season-inappropriate cut-off jeans, and a sleeveless, Surfin' U.S.A. shirt that could have been as old as the Beach Boys song, also greeted us. He was more formal than during our previous meeting as he shook our hands and introduced himself as Finley Livers, which explained the mildew-covered sign over the door that said *Livers*. Under it was a newer wooden sign that read: *LIVErs TO SURF*.

Finley waved us in. "Welcome to my humble abode."

Charles looked around. "Nice house."

Finley grinned. "Thanks, my granny left it to me. She owned it since the beginning of time. My parents are in California and didn't want it and my sister got a bunch of money from granny and lives in Houston."

Nosy Charles asked, "Live by yourself?"

"First floor," he said and nodded toward the ceiling. "Rent the upstairs to Ryan and Truman. We're all surfers." He yelled for us to hear him over the rock music blasting from deep in the house.

Charles looked toward the direction of the music and put his hands over his ears. "Neighbors ever comment on how much they like the music?"

Finley laughed. "Nah. Rentals on each side and in back. Seldom anyone's there." He lowered his voice. "Squatters sneak in, but they're in no position to complain. You the noise police?"

Charles made a faux gasp. "No way."

"Good," Finley said. "I didn't ask you here to talk about loud music. Come on back with the rest of the gang."

We followed Finley to a large sunroom that looked like a back porch that had been enclosed. There were ten mismatched chairs with seven of them occupied. Finley moved to the corner of the room and yanked the plug on a large, industrial-strength sound system. The smell of marijuana was stronger than it had been in the entry, but I didn't see the source.

The room turned silent, and most of the heads turned toward Charles and me. Someone mumbled, "The geezers have arrived." A couple of the others chuckled, and Finley moved to the center of the room.

"Folks, some of you know Chris, umm—"

"Landrum," I prompted.

Finley nodded. "And his friend Charles Fowler. They were at the meeting at the surf shop. Yell out who you are."

Two or three of them started talking, and Finley waved his arm. "One at a time."

"Teddye," said the young lady seated closest to me. I remembered her from the Dog and from the previous meeting.

Then the names flowed as smoothly as a choppy sea: Roscoe, Deb, Truman, Ryan, Todd, and the one face I was more familiar with, but still surprised to see, Dude's employee, Stephon.

After the introductions and my once again forgetting most of the names, Finley said, "Chris and Charles are here because of Dude. He said these two have caught more bad guys than all the police departments put together. Dude said if there's a crime, they'll solve it. He said, and I quote, 'They be best dee-tectives in galaxy.'"

Teddye giggled, and Stephon said, "Yep, it's what boss man said."

"Guys," Finley continued, "we're good surfers; we're good people. I've talked to each of you enough in the last few days to know you're bummed by the missing Baby Jesus. Some folks over here may not like us, heck, some think we're the scum of the earth. We love Folly and most of the time we love everyone's, well, most everyone's, tolerance and understanding. But, we don't know a pisspot full of, well, piss, about catching crooks. Stealing Jesus and the surfboards is a call to arms. It's why Chris and Charles are here."

He turned to the two of us. "We want to ask you what we can do to catch the scoundrel."

I wanted to duck behind one of the chairs. What did we have to offer? I glanced at Charles and waited for him to say something helpful. It was not to be.

"Gentlemen, and ladies," I said to fill the void. "We appreciate your concern and the invitation." Now, what do I say? "I don't have all the answers." I should have said I didn't have any of them. "I know a couple of things. You're taking turns watching the Nativity scene. That's great and will deter the thief from taking anything else."

"It don't get Jesus back," said the surfer to my right. I believe it was Todd.

"True, but it helps protect the Nativity. That's important."

One of the others said, "Do you have any idea who it was? Are there witnesses to any of it?"

"No, umm …"

"Truman," the questioner offered.

"No, Truman, as far as I know there were no witnesses."

Finley said, "Dude told me you'd catch him."

I smiled. "I wish I had his confidence."

"What else can we do?" Finley asked.

Charles stepped in front of me. "Abe Lincoln said, 'It's not me who can't keep a secret, it's the people I tell that can't.'"

A couple of them chuckled. Truman said, "Funny." I resisted rolling my eyes, and said, "What Charles means is people, even the worst crooks, tend to run their mouths. They get satisfaction from what they did and feel the need to tell someone." Jason and Samuel came to mind. "The main thing you can do is remain vigilant. You can keep your ears open. Somebody may be bragging about stealing the statue or the other things. Don't do anything stupid. If you hear something, call the police. It's their job; let them do it."

Finley repeated, "Anything else?"

I knew it was a stretch but figured I didn't have anything to lose by asking. "Do any of you know any less than honorable people who might buy the statue, possibly an antique dealer?"

Roscoe said, "Because we're surfers you assume we know crooks—thanks."

Finley leaned forward. "I don't think it's what he meant."

"Absolutely not, Roscoe," I said. "If we're going to find out what's going on, we have to look at everything. We figured the thief wants money, and if so, he would have to find someone to pay top dollar for the Baby Jesus. A pawnshop or your average low life may buy the surfboards and jewelry, but not the statue. I figured you're smart people and might know or have heard about shady antique dealers. I'm sorry if I offended you."

Roscoe sighed. "Yeah, right."

Deb waved her hand in the air like she had a question or had to go to the restroom. Finley nodded her direction, and she said, "My uncle owns Winslow's Antiques on King Street in Charleston. If you want, I'll call him and see if he knows anyone who might buy stolen stuff."

Charles said, "That'd be great, Deb. I'll give you Chris's number. You can also tell your Uncle Chris, and I may come a callin'."

"Anything else?" Finley said for the third time.

I shook my head, and Charles said, "Nope."

"That's all, Charles and Chris."

We were dismissed. Charles gave Deb my number, and he told her to call, day or night. Thanks, Charles.

Finley escorted us to the door and thanked us for coming. Inside, the sound system had been jacked up to the volume of a runaway freight train. On the way to the car, I noticed a light in the house next door. I hoped whoever it was had earplugs, but if it was a squatter, he probably couldn't afford them.

CHAPTER 12

The gods of winter had blessed Folly with a mild Friday so I walked to Cal's for a heart-unhealthy cheeseburger and to enjoy a few hours of country music. The temperature was mild, although I still needed a heavy jacket and winter Tilley. Two of the houses along the way were wrapped in Christmas lights. The sight reminded me of my dad driving mom and me around nearby subdivisions the week before Christmas and looking for the most colorful displays. A few of the years there was snow on the yards and roofs, and the colorful lights and wooden Santas and snowmen waved to us from the white lawns. I realized how old-fashioned I was since I preferred the low-tech displays with their large, colorful light bulbs rather than the LED displays that are common today. And, don't get me started on the ubiquitous blow-up decorations that may be attractive at night but during the day, when their inflating fans are off, look like Santa got run over by a steamroller.

I approached Cal's, smiled, and admitted most of my problems with today's decorations were because I was getting old and stuck in my ways. I smiled because I refused to get depressed over my rapid journey to Geezerland.

Friday nights in Cal's were festive. Locals and many

vacationers stopped by to enjoy the retro atmosphere, the retro country hits, and the retro owner who entertained. No one would count the weekend before Christmas as crowded, but most of the tables were full, and Cal was on stage in his retro-rhinestone coat, his Stetson, cowboy boots, and strumming his Martin acoustic guitar.

Cal was on the last notes of "Oh, Lonesome Me" as I moved to the only vacant seat at the bar. His spine curved toward the antique microphone. "Ladies and Gents, I'm a goin' to finish the set with one of my favorite songs from my dear friend, God rest his soul, Hank Williams Sr. Hope you like my version of "Hey, Good Lookin'." He winked at two white-haired ladies sitting at the table closest to the stage and began the song he had sung three thousand times. Kristin, who typically waited tables, was behind the bar while Cal put a glass of Cabernet in front of me before I could take off my coat and decide what I wanted. She, of course, got the drink right, and I told her I'd take a cheeseburger and fries. She said she could probably find them somewhere in the kitchen.

Cal finished the song. "Now, before I take a pause for the cause, I've got a request." He waved his hand at the crowd. "All of us are lucky. We have somewhere to hang our hats." He hesitated and touched the brim of his Stetson. "We have food, and many of us have our health and someone to share life with." He paused and shook his head. "But not everyone on Folly is that fortunate. Sad as it might be, we have our share of homeless. Yes, people who have to depend on the kindness of others to make it through these cold nights and keep food in their bellies. With Christmas rolling around next week, I'm taking up a special collection with the donated dough going to the homeless."

I looked around and with the exception of one table where a couple was more interested in texting, or whatever they were doing with their phones, everyone focused on Cal. "Now open your wallets. Open them wide. When I'm on my way to take a pis—umm, to powder my nose, I'm going to walk by your table and hold out my hat. Folks less fortunate than you'll appreciate your kindness. And I'm aging a bit and coins are heavy, so make sure you drop in lightweight paper money. Appreciate it."

Cal removed his Stetson, smoothed down his hair, and headed to the table where the white-haired ladies were rooting in their purses searching for lightweight paper money.

I sipped wine and looked to see who was here. I didn't notice them when I came in, but Charles and Preacher Burl were huddled at the table in the back corner. I told Kristin where I would be and maneuvered around two tables to visit my friends.

I tapped the preacher on the shoulder, and Charles said, "Wondering when you were going to stop ignoring us."

"Didn't see you. Hi, Preacher."

"Join us, Brother Chris," Burl said and pulled out the chair beside him.

I said, "Working on your sermon?"

Burl laughed. "Yes, Brother Chris. I'm thinking about adding some of Cal's tunes to my hymn selections."

"May attract more sinners," I said.

"No shortage already, Brother Chris."

Charles ignored us and had turned to the table behind ours and was talking to Finley, the surfer whose house we'd been to last night. The man with Finley was also at the meeting, but I didn't remember his name. The third person at the table was someone I didn't recognize. Charles held up his hand for Finley to stop whatever he was saying. Charles waved toward me. "Chris, you remember Finley and Truman don't you?"

I was getting older, but not senile, and said, "Hi, guys."

Finley waved at me. "Hey, Chris, meet Mary Ewing, a friend of ours."

Mary was in her early twenties, anorexic thin, with dirty blond hair, and a sad smile. She avoided my eyes and mumbled, "Pleased to meet you."

I said hi to Mary, and Finley and Truman resumed their conversation.

Charles leaned closer to their table. "Pull up a chair."

Finley looked at his friends and shrugged. "Sure." He slid their table close to ours. Burl moved his chair so the tables could touch. Mary scooted her chair closer but looked like she would rather not move.

Kristin arrived with my food, and Charles asked if the three newcomers wanted anything and said I was buying. Each said another drink would be nice.

Kristen headed to the bar at the same time Cal waved his Stetson in our faces. Burl, Truman, and I reached for our wallets. Charles didn't carry a driver's license and didn't have credit cards, so he had no use for a wallet, but pulled a twenty out of his pocket and dropped it in the hat. Burl and I did the same, and Finley started to add a five to the mix, hesitated, and said, "Where did you say the money was going?"

Cal hesitated, and said, "The needy."

Finley said, "Who decides?"

"That's a good question, my friend. I'm turning it over to Preacher Burl."

Burl put his arm on Finley's shoulder. "Brother, umm—"

The surfer said, "Finley Livers."

"Brother Finley, I'm Burl Ives Costello and preach at First Light Church. In good weather, we meet on the beach. In winter, our services are on Center Street."

Finley interrupted, "I've been a couple times. You're doing a fine job."

Burl looked closer at him like he was trying to remember. "Sorry, didn't recognize you. Anyway, at Sunday's service I'll be taking up a collection to provide food and warm clothing to needy families identified by my flock. Brother Cal has agreed to donate tonight's offering—collection—to what we get."

I interrupted and told the preacher that Finley and Truman were part of a group of surfers who're trying to find out who stole the Baby Jesus.

"Ah," Burl said. "So I've heard. God bless you. Please tell me if there is anything I can do to aid in your quest. I will be praying of course, but it may take more than that."

"Heard who did it?" Truman asked.

"Afraid not," Burl said. "I'm still hopeful it was a malicious prank, and the Baby Jesus will turn up."

Finley leaned closer to Burl. "I heard a rumor someone knew and told someone else a coven of witches took it. Wanted to ruin Christmas."

Burl looked at him. "I'm sure there are people with those inclinations, Brother Finley, but I don't put much credence in a rumor about someone telling someone who told someone—think I have it right."

Mary kept glancing around the room but smiled at Burl. "Reverend Costello, what time does church start?"

Burl returned her smile. "Sister Mary, call me Preacher Burl. We gather a few minutes before eleven and have fellowship around a container of lemonade, and as a concession to winter, coffee. The service begins at eleven. Shall you be joining us?"

She lowered her head again. "Are youngsters welcome?"

"Sister Mary, all are welcome. Do you have a child?"

She smiled. "Two, Preacher Burl. Jewel's six and Joanie just turned two."

"I'd love to see the three of you there."

Cal stood and leaned close to Burl. "My fans are getting antsy. Gotta start another set. Got something you can put this in?" He pulled the paper money out of his hat, turned each bill going the same direction, and handed it to Burl.

"Think it'll fit in my pocket. Thank you, Brother Cal." Burl looked down at the money. "This'll make some people mighty happy."

Finley leaned closer to Burl and pointed at the wad of cash. "Preacher, I sure hope you don't give the money to the places that always get it. I drive a truck for Quality Auto Parts and deliver stuff to repair shops. I'm always driving in alleys and behind stores and see people, homeless, I suppose, who don't have anywhere to go and stay in the shadows. My dad worked for a welfare agency back home and was always telling us about those forgotten folks—he called them the invisible ones.

Burl nodded. "Brother Finley, throughout my years in the ministry, I have seen, and gotten to know some of those to whom you refer. A few had too much pride to ask for help; others are so socially inept that they can't adjust to being around others; and, there are other reasons I can't think of now."

"That's who I'm talking about, Preacher Burl."

Burl held the cash in front of him. "Brother Finley, I assure you these generous donations will go to those in dire need."

Cal opened the set with Freddie Hart's "Trip to Heaven," and the noise in the bar increased as customers talked over the music. Kristin returned with the drinks, and Mary looked at her watch.

"The Lord Knows I'm Drinking," was next on Cal's playlist and we ran out of things to talk about. The surfers and Mary sipped their beers, and Charles tapped his bottle on the table in time with the music. Mary leaned forward. "I've got to get back to my gals."

Finley said he'd drop her off on his way to take the next shift at the Nativity. Truman stood and said he'd go to the Nativity with Finley.

Burl said, "I look forward to seeing you at our service Sunday."

Only Mary had said anything about attending.

Mary smiled, Finley shrugged, and Truman reminded Burl to not forget the needy.

"Nice folks," Charles said as they headed to the door.

And Cal, saying it was in the spirit of the Christmas season, started singing "Grandma Got Run Over By a Reindeer."

CHAPTER 13

The temperature on the last Saturday before Christmas was expected to struggle to reach the mid-forties with a light drizzle darkening the already gray day. I would have preferred to stay home, but realized even though I had made my semi-annual trek to Harris Teeter, I had little food in the house, and as the old saying goes, or should go, man can't live on fruitcake alone. I called Charles and asked if he wanted to meet for lunch at the Grill and Island Bar, a large restaurant that overlooked Center Street and was close to my friend's apartment. He said he could work it in his busy schedule and would meet me there.

The manager met me at the door. "Charles told me to tell you you're late and as usual he's waiting for you out there." He pointed to the patio.

Charles waved his watch-less wrist as I approached the booth located near a portable heater.

I got his meaning. "What'd you do, jog?"

"Jog," Charles laughed. "You're quite a jokester—a tardy jokester."

Dillon, a waiter whom I'd met on several other visits, was quick to the table and put me out of the misery of having to listen to Charles complain. I ordered a Coke, and Charles said, "Beer, any kind as long as it starts with Bud."

Charles watched Dillon leave and said, "It was nice of Cal to take up a collection. It'll help folks have a Christmas."

I agreed and asked, "Are you going to First Light tomorrow?"

"You bet."

Until Preacher Burl started First Light, Charles and I had probably attended church services about as often as a sea otter recites the Pledge of Allegiance. In the last few months, he has attended almost every week. Preacher Burl has a knack for reaching a wide range of people and making everyone feel welcome, regardless of social status or level of religious commitment.

Charles waited for Dillon to leave our drinks and continued, "Probably'll be a full house being close to Christmas and Burl's been telling everyone about the special offering."

As he was talking, I looked across the street and saw Jason and Samuel peddle up the sidewalk and turn on Indian Avenue. I hadn't realized I'd said anything when Charles said, "What's with *huh*?"

I pointed across the street. "Samuel and Jason. They're on their way to stake out the Nativity. They're determined to catch the thief and I'm afraid they may get in trouble." I told him about them following the UPS truck.

Charles took a sip of beer and chuckled. "Sounds like something we'd do."

We hadn't ridden around on bikes, but we had staked out a few spots, and had stumbled on some things we shouldn't have.

"True, although we're a tad older than those two, and more mature."

"Does tad mean a half century?"

I nodded.

"That's what I thought. Folks'd give you a powerful

argument against us being more mature."

"Either way, I worry about them."

Charles looked in the direction of the crèche. "What do you think the odds are on the thief trying to take something else?"

I looked across the street. "Low to nonexistent."

Charles nodded. "Church members, surfer group, and now Jason and Samuel. Mother and substitute child may be sleeping in heavenly peace, but they're being guarded more closely than Colonel Sanders' secret fried chicken recipe."

"It makes them feel like they're doing something to help."

Charles returned to his beer, took another sip, and looked at me. "So how're we going to catch him?"

I shrugged and looked up and saw Chief Cindy LaMond standing beside the booth and pointing at Charles's beer.

She wore a down jacket and jeans, so I figured she was off duty. "Want to join us?"

"If you'll scoot your lard ass over so I can fit in the booth."

Cindy had a way of making everyone around her feel good. I moved over, she sat, and Charles said, "Find Jesus?"

"Golly, Charles, I never knew you were interested in my salvation."

Charles huffed. "You know what I mean."

Cindy smiled. "Of course I do. The answer's no."

"Looking less like a prank," I said.

Cindy said, "You're right." She looked around to see if anyone was close enough to hear. No one was. "That's not the worst of it."

Charles leaned closer to the chief. "What?"

"At seventeen hundred hours, yesterday, a delivery truck left a package about the size of a shoebox on the porch at a house in the five hundred block of East Arctic, and—"

Charles interrupted—one of his better-honed talents, "What's with the seventeen hundred hours jabber? You forget how to talk English?"

"Practicing. Our mayor told me I needed to start speaking like a professional law enforcement official. Figured translating big and little hand time to military gobbledygook would confuse the citizenry enough to sound professional. You want to waste time talking about my vocabulary or listen to what I was saying?"

Brian Newman was the mayor and had been chief for many years before he was talked into running for his current position. He had appointed Cindy chief over a few officers with more seniority. He had said he wanted to shake things up in the force and Cindy was the person to do it. Brian was right. He also was a friend and father of Karen Lawson, the lady I had been dating.

Charles tilted his head to the left and to the right. "Continue."

"At eighteen hundred hours—six hours past noon to you citizen folk—the homeowner got home and went to the porch to get the package."

"And it was gone," Charles interrupted.

"Shut your pie hole. I'm telling the story."

He made a zipping his lips motion.

"Good," Cindy said. "And it was gone."

I stifled a chuckle. "What was it?"

"Don't suppose it was what the thief had hoped for. It was a box of printer ink cartridges, total retail value ninety-eight bucks. And it's worth that much only if you have a highfalutin color printer to stick them in. The point is, the thievin' continues."

Charles said, "No one saw the thief?"

"Sort of."

Charles rubbed his chin. "Sort of saw him, sort of didn't see him? Sort of what?"

Cindy gave an exaggerated nod. "Yep. Now where's

my beer." She turned and watched Dillon head our way.

We ordered more drinks and after a brief discussion, decided that since it was almost Christmas, our lunch could consist of sharing slices of Southern Pecan Pie, and Chocolate Lava Cake. Cindy was right to call me lard ass.

"Chief, did someone see the thief?" I asked to follow up on her less than illuminating comment.

"See, no; record, yes—sort of. A paranoid couple two houses down have security cameras all over their property. When the husband saw the police lights at the house with a printer and no ink, he came strolling up the street and announced he may have caught, in his words, 'the perp on camera.' To answer your question Charles, he sort of did. His camera wasn't close enough to catch much. All we could tell from the digital file—that's professional talk for what in your day was called tape—was that the thief was a male because of his height. We judged him to be five nine or ten."

Charles said, "Could have been a tall woman."

"It's possible, sir, although he lumbered away from the scene of the crime like a guy rather than like a graceful lady." She glared at Charles. "Now, back to my description, he wore a dark hoodie with the hood pulled up over his head. He appeared to be on foot since he ran out of the yard and away from the camera instead of hopping in a car."

"That's it?" Charles said.

"Affirmative, sir."

Dillon returned with our lunch and interrupted Cindy's professional cop-speak. Charles had a mouth-full of pecan pie, but it didn't stop him from asking, "Know any crooked antique dealers?"

Another of Charles's areas of expertise was changing verbal directions without giving a turn signal or concern for what others had been saying.

Cindy, being the lady in the group, swallowed a bite of lava cake, wiped a napkin across her lips, and squinted at

Charles. "Why? You steal a Roman pissing pot and want to turn it into cash."

"Umm, no," Charles said. "Just—"

Cindy snapped her fingers. "Don't tell me. You think whoever stole Baby Jesus will try to sell it, and no pawn shop will give him much, and no reputable antique dealer will want to put his white glove-covered pinkie on it."

Cindy wasn't chief only because of her pretty face and uncanny ability to shake-up the establishment.

Charles said, "Yes."

Cindy took another bite and said, "And you think you're smarter than the police and figured that out all by yourself while the cops are sitting around counting our toes?"

"Never."

Cindy said, "Mongoose manure."

"Mongoose?" Charles said.

"Charles, for your personal edification—how's that for professional?"

Charles said, "Move on, Chief."

Cindy smiled. "For your edification, at thirteen hundred hours yesterday—hell, I'm confusing myself. One o'clock yesterday, one of my guys contacted the sheriff's office to see if they were aware of antique dealers who may lean toward the wrong side of the law." Cindy took another bite of cake.

I waited, knowing she would tell us what she had learned. Charles, who counted patience as one of the deadly sins, said, "And?"

"And this is good cake. Stuff your mouth with some, Charles, so I can finish talking."

Charles stared at the chief.

"And the detective who specializes in that sort of thing is on a Christmas vacation with his family somewhere where Christmas trees look like cactuses. The guy my officer spoke to, said he wasn't aware of any crooked dealers, but would call the cactus man and ask him to call us."

Once again, Charles looked at his wrist. "He hasn't called you yet?"

"Charles, I'm off today and don't know."

"You've got to find out, so—"

Cindy waved her hand in Charles's face, sighed, and grabbed her phone.

"Is Officer Spencer around?" she asked after a long delay before someone answered. There was another delay and she said, "Have him call me ASAP, stat, or whatever our cop code number is for *now*." She hit end call and rubbed her forehead. "This pro-cop crap is giving me a headache."

I said, "Cindy, if the thief's trying to sell the statue, crooked antique dealers would be only one source. There're collectors who'd have an interest. How would we find them?"

Cindy moved her hand from her head. "We?"

"Meaning you."

"Right. Anyway, I asked Spencer to ask the detective that when he calls from vacationland. It's a long shot. I'm afraid it'll take a heap of luck for us to find Baby Jesus. I hate it for Preacher Burl, and to be honest, everyone here. A lot of folks who don't know the preacher or who don't attend his, or any church, but they look at the stealing of the statue as a personal affront to all who love Folly." She shook her head. "Gotta run some errands for hubby. He hasn't managed to get out of the store since I don't know when. It's revolting how many toilet plungers he sells this time of year."

It was more than I wanted to know.

Charles said, "But—"

Once again, Cindy stuck her hand in his face. "Charles, as soon as I learn anything from the vacationing detective, I will not take another breath without calling to give you the scoop. Of course, you won't be home and since you're too cheap to buy an answering machine or one of these new inventions called a cell phone, I'll call Chris."

"That'll do."

Cindy put on her coat. "Good, because that's all you'll get." She headed to the exit.

Charles and I accomplished two things. First, we gained seventy pounds from stuffing ourselves with the rest of the holiday season entrees. Second, Charles decided we should go to Charleston and stop at antique shops and see if we could learn if they knew of any crooked ones. I had learned years ago once Charles was on a mission, little, if anything, could stop him. Instead of asking how he had planned to get this information, or what he planned to do with it if he was able to learn anything, I said I'd pick him up Monday morning. We did know one antique dealer to talk to.

CHAPTER 14

First Light's foul weather sanctuary was on Center Street in a storefront next to my gallery. Christmas was the prime selling season for most retailers, but with so few vacationers here, and the apparent shortage of residents who couldn't live without having my photographs adorning their walls, I hadn't bothered to open the last two weekends and had taped a note on the door saying: *Open by Appointment*, along with my phone number. I hadn't received any calls, so at least I wasn't stuck in the gallery waiting for desperate buyers. I would miss having the gallery, but was looking forward to not having to consistently write checks that far exceeded its revenue.

A generous benefactor had donated money for the church to rent the space and remodel and members of Burl's flock had spent hours converting the long-vacant retail shop into a place to hold services. Before they had the storefront, Burl was forced to cancel services during inclement weather.

I arrived fifteen minutes before the service was scheduled to begin, and was surprised by the large number of people already there. The room only held fifty, and it was full. Preacher Burl was near the door and talking to Mel and Caldwell, two friends of mine. He saw me and patted Mel on the back and pointed him toward the coffee urn at the front of the sanctuary. Mel and Caldwell headed to the liquid refreshments, and Burl welcomed me.

"Great turnout," I said.

"God has been good to us this morning. I have spread the word all week about taking a special collection and," he hesitated and waved his hand around the room, "several have come for that reason." He grinned. "Of course, they also desire to hear the word of the Lord, and, to be honest, the last Sunday before the day celebrating the birth of Jesus Christ, brings out the twice a year church goers."

Lottie, who had attended since the beginning and who had put in hours of manual labor fixing up the building, tapped the preacher's arm. "Preacher Burl, the coffee pot needs your delicate touch. Sorry, Brother Chris, I must borrow our leader."

I told her it was fine and looked around. Charles was in front of the room talking to Dude, Finley, Truman, and Deb. Roscoe was off to the side looking uncomfortable. I hadn't seen any of them here before. I barely recognized Bernard, the homeless man to whom Cal had introduced me. He had slicked back his hair, and had on a clean dress shirt, but the same slacks he had worn when he was in Cal's. He was talking to the tall, lanky singer who attended as seldom as Finley and his crew. Stephon, from the surf shop, was by himself and seated in the back pew, and there were several couples I recognized from other services but didn't know their names. A few others I didn't know were milling around.

Preacher Burl fiddled with the coffee pot and looked at his watch. He walked to an old lectern that had spent its better years in a high school gymnasium and cleared his throat. He didn't get the results he'd wanted, so he cleared it again; this time much louder, and said, "Please repose thyselves." He pointed to the pews.

Several of his flock moved toward the pews; a few, probably those here for the first time, looked at him like

"Repose thyselves?" Everyone moved to a seat. By habit, I headed to the back pew, but before I was seated, the door opened, and Mary looked in. She spotted me and I waved for her to enter. She stepped outside and seconds later she tiptoed in followed by two children. I slid to the center of the pew so there was room for them. The children's clothes fit poorly and had been mended in multiple places.

Preacher Burl raised both hands over his head. "Please silence thy portable communication devices."

To say he religiously began each service with those words, would be sacrilegious, but regardless, he had. To make sure newcomers understood his meaning, he waved his cell phone over his head.

Burl led us in the first hymn, and because of a shortage of vocal talents, he stopped after two verses. William Hansel, a close friend and regular at First Light, was out of town and unable to lend his incredible singing voice to the congregation. Burl shared what led up to the birth of the baby Jesus that I suppose is a ministerial requirement this close to Christmas. The children began to wiggle in their seats and look around but weren't talking. Each time one of them started to stand, Mary touched the child's arm and nodded at the seat. I was impressed how well behaved they were.

After another failed attempt for the group to carry a tune, Burl reached under the pulpit—lectern—and pulled out a wicker basket. "Brothers and sisters, as many of you know, we are privileged to be able to come out on such a chilly morn, healthy enough to get here on our own, and from the looks of some of us, have no shortage of nourishment." Burl patted his ample stomach and chuckled. "For many, some here on Folly, food and shelter are luxury items and outside their reach. Can we feed, clothe, and shelter all of God's creatures who are less fortunate? No, but what we can do is to identify the most needy and give them some light on their Christmas morning, a toy for the most innocent of children, and food to nourish their stomach and spirit."

Burl bowed his head and gave us a moment for his message to sink in. He raised the basket. "Now is time for us to do our share. Please reach deep in your pockets and help brighten someone's Christmas. While Sister Lottie walks among you so you can contribute, I will tell you how we have selected the recipients of this love offering." He handed Lottie the basket. "I've named a small group from our flock, headed by Brother Dennis Richardson, a social worker with ties to local charities, to determine where our contributions will go. He's identified two such charities and with agreement from the other members of the group, will be dividing your givings between the two."

I glanced at Mary and her two children and wondered if she would receive some of the money or the food it would buy. I also saw her open a small purse with a broken zipper and pull out a wadded dollar bill and three coins. She handed the dollar to the oldest child, and the change to the youngest and whispered something to each of them. Lottie reached our pew and each child smiled and dropped the money in the basket. I turned my head to keep from tearing up.

Lottie returned to the front of the room and handed the basket to Burl, and he looked in and smiled. "Praise the Lord. You have made Christmas a time to rejoice for those in need. I thank you." He led the flock in singing "Joy to the World."

Maybe the spirit of the Lord was present. Our singing sounded decent.

***

Charles, Lottie, and I stayed after the service to help Burl clean the sanctuary. Lottie was in her forties and had been beautiful in her younger days, but life's trials and tribulations had taken its toll. She was still attractive, but wore baggy clothes to disguise her trim figure, and her dark-brown hair had seldom met a brush. We'd met the first time I'd met Burl when she and a couple of other volunteers were renovating the space. Today she wore newer clothes than usual and had made an effort with her hair.

She was in good spirits as she cleaned up around the coffee pot. "How'd we do, Preacher?"

Burl rested the basket on his lectern and had counted the donations. "Sister Lottie, we have 275 reasons for which to be thankful."

"Wonderful, Preacher Burl," Lottie said and hugged him.

There had been speculation Lottie was "sweet on" Burl, but if it was true, no one had offered proof. She had credited him with turning her life around, and she never missed a service, but it was all anyone knew.

"Yes," Burl said. "Add the $150 donated Friday evening by the fine patrons of Cal's, and we can give $425 to Brother Dennis to distribute."

Charles had been folding chairs, which had been added to the room to accommodate the crowd. He finished and said, "Preacher Burl, Lottie, could Chris and I take you to lunch to celebrate?"

Translated, it meant could we take you and Chris will pick up the check.

Burl looked at Lottie and at Charles. "Brother Charles, have you known me to turn down a meal?"

Charles smiled.

"And where shall we break bread for our celebratory meal?"

"The Dog," Charles said. "Lottie, join us?"

She shook her head. "I need to finish, there's still cleaning to do."

Burl said, "You can do it later. Why don't you come?"

She grinned. "That sounds nice."

Burl put the money in a small lockbox and put it in

the bottom drawer of the old metal desk. Lottie and Burl walked side-by-side with Charles and me following. The Dog was packed; members of Folly's other churches occupied most of the tables. We took a table that had just been vacated, and Amber was there with menus as soon as we were seated. Burl said water when asked for our drink order; the rest of us followed suit. Amber didn't make eye contact with me the entire time.

"Preacher, that was a fine message this morning," Lottie said. "Christmas is such a wonderful time, especially for youngsters."

"Thank you, Sister Lottie. I hope the offering will bring smiles to some children and food to their stomachs."

She smiled and twisted her hair around a finger. I was beginning to think Charles and I should move to another table. Maybe she was sweet on the preacher.

Charles didn't take kindly to being left out. "Preacher, what was Christmas like for you as a child?"

Burl looked at Lottie and turned to Charles. "I once told you I grew up on a cattle farm in Illinois. I confess church wasn't big on my parents' agenda and we seldom attended." He stopped and smiled. "The Christian Church in town had a grand Nativity scene, one of those living ones where real people played characters from the Bible. There were animals in the scene, and one of the deacons came to dad and asked if he could furnish a couple of cows. There weren't a lot of donkeys around and finding a camel in our neighborhood was out of the question." He laughed. "Dad didn't want to. He grumbled and said his cows had more important things to do than be actors."

Lottie must have been taking lessons in impatience from Charles. "What happened?"

Burl smiled. "Mom wasn't having any of it, and she told dad Christmas only came once a year, and she figured we could do without the cows for five nights. Dad gave in but said someone had to be with his animals at the Nativity.

I remember him stomping his foot on the floor and saying he wasn't going to be the one so mom said I could do it and it'd be good for me. I wasn't certain how it would be good."

Lottie put her hand on Burl's arm. "That's sweet. Did you do it?"

"It wasn't how I would have chosen to spend those long, cold, pitch-black nights, but if mom said it was what I was doing, it was what I was doing. It turned out I was glad I did and continued the tradition the next two Christmas seasons. Each night, dad would truck us to the Nativity but wouldn't get out, so I had to get the animals over to the scene. Most of the time the cows seemed bored by it all, but I watched the people from all over town as they inched close to the Nativity. They treated it with so much reverence that I was amazed." He shook his head. "To me, it just seemed like a bunch of people dressed up like they did in the old days and stood around the manger. To see the kids holding their parents' hands and tiptoeing closer to see Baby Jesus was something else. Some adults fell to their knees in prayer. It was life altering."

Charles asked, "Was it a real baby?"

"No one thought it would be a good idea to place a live child in the manger, but the baby was the only thing that wasn't real. I was fifteen the first time and didn't understand the impact the dressed-up people and animals had on people who came to see it. Heck, I'd been around cows my entire life and didn't see anything special about them other than giving us milk and stepping on my foot when I wasn't careful."

I asked, "Is that why you wanted to have First Light's Nativity, and were so upset when the Baby Jesus was taken?"

"Brother Chris, watching those people left a lifelong impression on me. I almost cried long ago when Christmas Eve arrived, and we stopped doing the Nativity. When I found my way to God years later, I told myself if I was able to help facilitate such a symbolic representation of what happened all those hundreds of years ago, I would." He pointed to the door. "There aren't a lot of cows on Folly, and sheep are in short supply, so I bought the plastic ones so we could have the Nativity. When Brother Robert offered us the Baby Jesus and told me its story, I'm not ashamed to say, I was ecstatic."

Charles said, "You'd also be hard-pressed to find three wise men around here. Present company excluded."

Burl laughed, accomplishing Charles's intent. The preacher turned serious. "I suppose it answers why it is so important." He lowered his head. "And now I feel like someone stuck a dagger through my heart. I know a carved piece of wood is only wood, but it means much more."

Amber arrived with our drinks and took our food order. She only looked my way when she asked what I wanted. I couldn't understand how she could be so angry about whatever she thought I told Jason and encouraged him to do.

Amber left to put in our order, and Lottie said, "Preacher Burl, the Baby Jesus you were given may be missing, but there's the one the kind man from the Methodist Church lent us, and look at all the good you've done this Christmas. Look at today's collection and the money from Cal's. Look at all the people you've touched over the year. You've done good."

"Thank you, Lottie." He asked each of us what we were doing Christmas.

We shared our plans, as meager as they were. Amber arrived with lunch and all conversation stopped. Burl told us how much preaching increased his appetite and patted his stomach as if we wouldn't figure out where the food was headed. Lottie shared that before Burl and his ministry had come into her life, she had gone days wondering where her next meal was coming from. She said he had given her faith and miraculously a bounty of food had followed. Burl was quick to point out it wasn't he but was the Lord who had provided. Again, she gently touched his arm.

Burl reminded us about the Christmas Eve service. "I'd prefer to hold it at midnight, but am in touch with my flock enough to know if I waited that late, I'd be talking to myself, and maybe a couple of our loveable intoxicated citizens." He smiled. "It's why I told everyone seven would be a good time." From the pulpit—lectern—he had said seven and if the weather was decent, the service would be on the beach. He nodded and looked at Charles and at me. "You will be joining me in sharing the blessed word of the birth of our Savior, won't you?"

"Of course," I said as if there could have been any other answer. Charles nodded, and Lottie said, "You know I will, Preacher Burl."

We spent a few minutes trying to remember what the weather gurus had said would be the temperature Christmas Eve. None of us knew, and Burl said God would be in control and hoped he blessed us with warmth.

Lottie was the first to finish and said she wanted to get back and finish straightening up the church. We thanked her for taking time to share a meal with us and she said it was her pleasure. She hugged Preacher Burl, and said she would see us Christmas Eve.

People who had just met him often underestimated Charles. Some people laugh at his ever-changing college T-shirt and sweatshirt wardrobe. Some find it curious that he constantly carries a handmade cane, while no one had been able to get an explanation why—me included. Strangers who saw him walking around town often thought he was one of the area's homeless. And, many of his conversations drifted south of normal. I must admit, when I first met him, I would have agreed. Okay, I admit, he's still quirky, although he's one of the most perceptive and sensitive people I've ever met.

Charles watched Lottie leave and turned to Burl.

"You two an item?"

Burl looked at Charles like he had accused him of being a warlock. "Brother Charles." The preacher's eyes opened wide, and he leaned back in the chair. "Why would you say that?"

"Preacher, even one of your dad's cows could see Sister Lottie's hankering to become a preacher's wife."

"Brother Charles, don't you think Sister Lottie is being appreciative for all First Light has done for her? It's nothing more than that."

Charles shook his head. "Preacher, I believe I can sum up my answer in two letters: NO."

Burl started to interrupt, and Charles stopped him. "Preacher, there's no doubt she's appreciative." Charles glanced at Burl's arm where Lottie had placed her hand more than once. "Get your nose out of your Bible and look around. Those touches and the look in her eyes say a heap more than appreciation."

Burl looked at his arm and back at Charles. "Heavens, I'm her preacher."

Charles said, "Preacher, I haven't spent a lot of time researching the mating habits of clergy, but it seems unless you're a Catholic priest—which I'm fairly certain you ain't—and maybe some other religions I'm not aware of, courtin', kissin', and marryin' are fairly common."

Burl leaned closer to the table and glanced around to see if anyone else was listening. "I must confess, Brother Charles, I find Sister Lottie, Miss Lottie, attractive and I know we share similar beliefs on many things, but—"

Charles leaned closer to Burl. "Preacher, unless the *but* you're going to say is *but* you don't know what preacher you could get to perform your wedding, I don't want to hear it. I would advise you to give serious thought to talking to Lottie about your feelings." Charles nodded. "I think a June wedding would be nice."

And that was marriage advice from someone who

had never been married; someone who had asked Heather to marry him; and from someone who had called it off.

Burl didn't get a chance to respond. Lottie charged in the restaurant, her face red, and tears in her eyes.

"It's gone!"

CHAPTER 15

All eyes turned to Lottie, who stumbled and tripped over a table near the door. The room got quiet as she regained her balance and approached us. Burl stood and wrapped his arms around her and eased her in the chair she had vacated minutes earlier.

"What's gone?" Burl asked, although I suspected he knew.

Lottie's shoulders sagged, she rested her elbows on the table, and put her head between her hands. "Christmas is gone. Hope for the needy, gone. Oh, Preacher, it's all gone."

Amber had returned and squatted down beside Lottie. "Can I get you water?"

Lottie mumbled, "Please."

I said, "What happened?"

Burl put his arm around Lottie who looked up with tears in her eyes. "Back door's open. Drawer smashed. The money's gone—it's gone."

Amber was quick with the water, and Lottie took a sip. I asked Amber for the check, paid, and said we should go to the church. It was cold outside, but I felt colder inside as we rushed to First Light. We entered the sanctuary, and I suggested Lottie may be more comfortable waiting on the back pew while Burl, Charles, and I continued to the office. The lockbox was on the floor, open, and empty. The back door looked like someone had used a crowbar on it. I told Charles and Burl not to touch anything and called Chief LaMond.

Five minutes later, the chief entered followed by Officer Allen Spencer, whom I'd known for several years. Cindy wore jeans, a paint-stained sweatshirt, and an old leather jacket. Spencer's six-foot frame was decked out in a crisp Folly Beach Department of Public Safety uniform with a matching coat.

"Thanks for coming," I said and pointed to the back room.

Cindy nodded and walked to the office door and looked around before turning to Spencer. "Start processing everything." He nodded and left the building.

"He'll get a print kit," Cindy said, and sat in the pew in front of us and turned to Burl. "What happened, Preacher?"

Burl told her about the special collection, how much was in it plus the money from Cal's, and about Lottie coming to the Dog to tell us. He said it was all he knew. Cindy turned to Lottie and in a softer voice asked what had happened. Lottie added little since all she had done was return to the sanctuary, saw the empty lockbox, and ran to the restaurant. Spencer returned and headed to the office.

Burl had his arm around Lottie and was reassuring her it wasn't her fault, and everything would be okay. A few minutes later, the officer rejoined us and was shaking his head. "There're some prints, probably yours Preacher, but most of them are smudged over. Looks like he wore gloves." He looked around. "Security cameras?"

Burl shook his head.

"Lottie," Cindy said, "I know the thief came in the back door but did you see anyone when you were coming here or after you found the box? There could have been more than one of them."

Lottie blinked. "An older couple was walking on the sidewalk when I got here. When I ran to the restaurant, I was so shook that I was lucky not to get run down crossing the street. I didn't see anyone. Sorry."

Spencer took Burl and Lottie's prints to compare to the ones on the box and Cindy asked him if anyone had been acting suspicious or curious about the collection. He shook his head. Cindy asked who would have known the money was there.

Burl hesitated and said, "Lord help me for saying this, but I would think everyone who attended the service would have known. They wouldn't know how much other than it was a decent amount considering the size of the flock."

Cindy asked if he would make a list of everyone he remembered being at the service. Burl said he would and asked Lottie and me to help with the list. Cindy told him to take his time and to call when it was finished, and she'd send someone to pick it up. She also said there wasn't anything else she and Officer Spencer could do but did offer to send Larry to repair the door.

"Sorry about this, Preacher," Cindy said and headed out.

I asked Burl if there was anything Charles and I could do. He said no, he wanted to be alone. I told him to call if he thought of anything or needed help with the names. He said he would. Charles and I left; Lottie stayed. Burl didn't want to be completely alone.

I closed the sanctuary door and realized I was fuming. It wasn't a huge sum of money, but I could still picture Mary's girls smiling as they contributed. The money represented the generosity of many, and several had given more than they could afford. This was now personal, and I had to do something.

I wasn't the least surprised when Charles stopped in

the middle of the sidewalk. "We've got to find the thief, got to get the money back, and got to find Baby Jesus."

Saying it was easier than doing it. We went in the gallery to get out of the cold and decided all we could do was to do what we'd already decided: talk to Deb's uncle, to see if he knew any crooked antique dealers.

***

I was becoming as impatient as Charles. I was sitting at my kitchen table, and it was only six thirty, Monday morning. I stared at the clock annoyed that it would be more than three hours before Winslow's Antiques opened. Charles had insisted I pick him up at nine so we could be at the store at ten. As usual, it was lost on him that with normal traffic, the trip would take twenty minutes.

Not able to make the time go quicker by staring at the clock, I walked to Bert's to grab a Danish and cup of complimentary coffee. Not only was the coffee free, so was a pleasant conversation with Eric, the store's well-known employee, conversationalist on topics both large and small, and wearer of one of the most distinct beards to be found in the Low country.

Eric waited for me to get coffee before he said, "Chris, hear about the theft at First Light?"

Eric wasn't as well-versed in the town's gossip as Amber or Charles, but since Bert's never closes, word of most everything that happens on the island walks through its doors. The affable employee never hesitated to listen to the ramblings of his customers.

"Afraid so, I was with Preacher Burl when he heard about it."

"Sorry," he said. "Lisa and I were talking about it last night. Stealing stuff off porches, absconding with the Baby Jesus, and now taking money for the homeless. It seems someone is trying to suck the spirit of Christmas out of our community."

Lisa was Eric's wife and another of Bert's employees. "Hear rumors about who might be responsible?"

Eric ran his hand over his beard. "Bum, Satanist, surfer, drug addict, run of the mill thief, ghost of Christmas past, jealous preacher from another church—I've heard them all. Ask me if I believe any of them." Eric didn't wait for my answer. "Not a one. If you ask me, it's someone who's needing quick cash for the holidays. Someone with a mess of youngins wantin' to give them a decent Christmas." He hesitated and looked at the double doors leading outside. "Chris, I feel horrible for First Light and especially Preacher Burl. He's a wonderful man doing great things for folks who don't fit in at other churches. I'm not condoning the thieving, but I also feel bad for the person doing it. If I'm right about the children, I feel worse for them."

"I agree, and Eric, could you do me a favor?"

He smiled. "As long as it doesn't get me killed."

"It won't. Could you give me a call if you hear anything that seems more credible than a ghost?"

Eric cocked his head to the side. "You meddling in police business again?"

I grinned. "Yes."

"Good. You're the most interesting neighbor this store's ever had. Good luck, and try not to get yourself dead."

I paid for the Danish, said I'd try not to get *dead*, and headed out as a man being dragged by two Dalmatians entered the store. And it was still before seven o'clock.

It was a mild morning, so instead of heading home and staring at the clock, I walked three blocks to the Folly Pier, sat on one of the wooden benches in front of Locklear's Restaurant, and ate breakfast. The pier was deserted, and the walkway was illuminated with amber lights set at intervals along the railings. The lights reminded me of Christmas and the deserted pier made me think of how empty the holiday would be for so many without the happiness the donated money could bring.

Three hardy surfers were trying to catch an early-morning wave, and two couples walking their dogs on the beach. The sun had peeked over the horizon and there wasn't a cloud to be seen. I saw a few stars before the light from the sun overpowered them. My mind wandered back to my childhood and the most memorable of all the church services I attended. And, although I had trouble remembering what I had for supper last night, the words to "Silent Night" were as clear as the breaking morning light.

Silent night, holy night,
Son of God, love's pure light;
Radiant beams from Thy holy face.
With the dawn of redeeming grace,
Jesus, Lord at Thy birth.

Yes, Eric, I said out loud. I am butting in. I must.

CHAPTER 16

Charles paced the crushed gravel and shell parking lot in front of his apartment. He glanced at his wrist and announced I was late. It was lost on him I was there when he told me to be. He hopped in the car and unzipped his jacket so I could see his long-sleeve sweatshirt. The green shirt had the head of a ram in the center with Colorado State above it.

He patted his chest and said, "Reminded me of the animals in the Nativity. Thought it'd round up enough psychic energy to find the slime bucket who bought Baby Jesus."

He'd said it with a straight face, so I suspected it was spoken with a kernel of sincerity. Charles had been spending too much time around his girlfriend Heather, who prided herself on being psychic and a country music singer. Her psychic powers exceeded her singing ability, but if you'd heard her sing, you would know that didn't mean squat.

"It looks as much like the sheep in the Nativity as you look like a porpoise."

"Symbolism, my literal friend, symbolism. Did you know the Magi, those three wise dudes who brought gifts, didn't show up until days, maybe months, after Jesus was in the manger?"

"Interesting," I said, which was often enough to get him to move to another topic.

"My point, ye of lesser biblical knowledge, is that the sheep could have been rams. You're old, although not old enough to have been hanging out at the stable, so you don't know what was there."

I rolled my eyes. "Yes, your shirt will help."

Charles grinned like he'd won a major victory.

King Street was home to some of Charleston's finest shops, ranging from well-known clothiers, to gift shops, to high-end jewelry stores. It also had the city's highest concentration of antique stores, with the most well-known being George C. Birlant & Co. Deb's uncle's store, Winslow's Antiques, was across the street and a half block south of Birlant. As predicted, we were standing in front of the historic building with Winslow's Antiques painted in script on the window when a man unlocked the door. He was in his seventies, five foot six, and better dressed than his visitors. He wore a dark-brown, three-piece wool suit, a starched white shirt, and a green and blue rep tie. He recovered from the surprise of seeing two men standing at his door, and looked us over like he was trying to decide if we were there to rob him. I would have done the same if a stranger looking like Charles had appeared at my door.

I stepped in front of Charles and extended my hand to the leery shopkeeper. "I'm Chris Landrum, and this is my friend Charles Fowler. We're from Folly Beach and your niece, Deb." I paused, realizing I didn't know her last name and had also assumed the man standing in front of us was Mr. Winslow. "She said you may be able to help us."

"Ah," he said. "Yes, she's a sweet girl, albeit a bit misguided. She called the other night and said there was a chance you might be stopping by. I apologize for my rudeness. I'm Saul, please come in."

The smell of dust, wood polish, and antiques assailed me as we moved past a row of dressers and tables halfway

106

through the store to a desk that served more than an item for sale. It was covered by invoices and handwritten notes. There was a laptop on the back corner, but its top was closed and covered with a layer of dust. On the laptop was a cordless phone and a coffee mug with *When Did I Become an Antique?* printed on it. Perhaps there was a sense of humor inside the starched shirt.

Saul pulled up two frail looking chairs from a dining room set behind us and motioned for us to sit.

He waited for us to be seated before saying, "Could I interest you gentlemen in a cup of hot tea?"

We said no.

"Misguided how?" Charles asked.

Charles wasn't about to let the comment about Saul's niece go unexplained.

"Her parents are not as traditional as the rest of our family. They live on a small farm outside Summerville and raise miniature horses—sell some, show some. Their goal is to live, umm, how do they describe it, off the grid with few connections with the outside world. As is the case with most people in contemporary America, they are not always successful. I'll leave it as they march to the beat of a different drummer." He paused and fiddled with a sheet of paper on the desk. "Are either of you fond of antiques?"

"I'm fond of Chris. Does that count?"

Saul chuckled. "I reached that vaulted status years earlier than your friend."

"How again is Deb misguided?" Charles said, although I didn't recall Saul saying how the first time.

"She came along later in my brother's life. He had already raised a family, and poor Deb received much less attention than her three siblings. I suppose it contributed to her drifting."

"Drifting?"

"Shall I say a more nomadic life? She doesn't appear amenable to settling down and from what I've seen, her friends share her alternative lifestyle."

"Like what?" Charles persisted.

"Perhaps drugs, perhaps not following the more defined mores of marriage and family. Don't get me wrong, she's a sweet lass, and I haven't had enough contact with Deb to understand her motivations. How well do you know her?"

"Hardly at all," I said. "We've met her twice and only talked to her once. She does seem nice."

"She's generous to a fault, always for the underdog and every lost cause. She has little, but would give whatever she has to anyone in need, and if possible, she'd take in any stray animal and any stray person. I can't tell you how many times she's requested I donate to one cause or another. I love her for it, and have given to some of them. I think her friends share her sensitivity to underdogs." He hesitated and held up his hand, palm facing Charles. "I know it's not why you're here. Deb told me about the purloined antique, a hand-carved statue of the Christ Child. A terrible situation. She said your theory was the person who walked away with it may try to sell it to a dealer of questionable repute. Is that correct?"

"It is," I said and explained about its value and why we didn't think it could be sold to a pawnshop.

"Logical," Saul said. "And you are asking me if I'm aware of unethical dealers."

I nodded.

"It puts me in an awkward conundrum. As you can imagine, I don't want to get anyone in trouble, and anything I say is based on hearsay."

I glanced at Charles and said, "Anything you tell us will be kept in confidence. All we are interested in is getting the antique back."

Saul looked at the paper he had been fiddling with. "As you may, or may not know, this stretch of King Street is known as the Antique District of Charleston. There are ten or more established dealers within a few hundred yards of us. Of course, not all dealers are located on King Street. Some are on East Bay, Savannah Highway, and others dot the county. The premiere dealers are no further from here than you could mallet an antebellum croquet ball."

"Crooked dealers?" Charles said.

"Now I'm not saying they're crooked per se, although there are two individuals you might want to take a closer look at." He sighed. "Are you sure this will go no further?"

I couldn't make that promise, but hedged by saying, "Your information is safe with us."

"I gave the question some thought after Deb's call. If I were looking for an antique of questionable provenance—which of course I am not, nor will I ever—I would consider shopping at Harold Lee's Antiques or possibly Arnold's Antique Barn. Mind you, I have no proof. I hope that helps."

I thanked him and got directions to the two stores.

"Be sure to tell Deb I asked about her. She's such a sweet young lady."

I told him I would as he walked us out.

***

Harold Lee's Antiques was off Savannah Highway in a strip center that was in dramatic contrast from the historic structures along King Street. It was built in the 1970s and from the worn lettering on the side of the building, it had been home to multiple tenants. From the outside, Harold Lee's Antiques looked more like a flea market than a reputable antique store. What it did share with Winslow's Antiques was the smell of dust and furniture polish. Also like Winslow's, this Monday in December was not a busy time for antique shoppers. Charles and I were greeted by the only other person in the building, a man in his mid-forties with the smile of a used-car salesman. He wore jeans and a white dress shirt and said he was Harold Lee, owner, as if we wouldn't know Harold Lee owned Harold Lee's Antiques.

"Welcome. It's nice to see customers so bright and early. As the saying goes, the early bird may get the worm, but it's the second mouse that gets the cheese." He laughed like it was the funniest thing he'd ever said. It may have been, but I wasn't amused. Charles and I smiled.

"Anyway," he continued after the moment of hilarity, "What may I interest you in this morning?"

It wouldn't be wise to say we wondered if he bought a stolen Baby Jesus, so I began a story we had crafted on the way to the store. "My friend and I inherited a collection of wooden statues my grandmother had said were hand carved a century ago in Germany. We have fallen in love with their intricate details and were looking to expand our collection."

Charles added, "There are several life-size pieces in the collection. Amazing, simply amazing. Would you by chance have similar items we could consider procuring?"

I wondered if we sounded sincere, or just gay.

Harold gave another car-salesmen smile. "I might have the perfect piece for your collection. It came in late last week, and I haven't had time to inventory it and to put it in the showroom. Pardon me a moment and I'll get it."

"Yes," Charles said as soon as Harold was out of hearing range.

No, I thought moments later when Harold returned with a giant smile and an equally giant carved eagle. It was life size, and no doubt valuable, but by no stretch of the imagination could it be confused with Baby Jesus. Charles made an audible sigh and I faked a smile as Harold held the eagle up for us to admire.

Harold quoted a price and said, "I'm sure this one-of-a-kind replica of our nation's symbol, would make a perfect addition to your collection."

"Excellent," I lied. "It's lovely." I ran my hand over its outstretched wing. "Do you have any other pieces we could combine with the eagle to possibly get a better price?"

Larger dollar signs may move him along.

"I wish I did," he said. "This is all I have."

"Too bad," Charles said. "Oh, by the way, the other day I ran into another collector. He said he had bought a statue of Jesus out of an antique Nativity scene. He had to leave before I got his name." Charles turned to me. "We wanted to see who he is so we could see his collection. Did you, by chance, sell him the piece?"

Excellent question, Charles.

"Sorry, no. I don't know who you were speaking to. But I'll tell you what, because it's Monday, a slow day in the store," he waved his hand around the empty store. "I'll give you a twenty-percent discount on this impeccable carving."

Charles said, "My friend and I will discuss it and get back with you."

Harold's smile seemed forced. "Of course, the discount will end at closing today."

Charles smiled. "We'll get back with you this afternoon."

Now, he'd lied.

We left Harold smiling at the possibility of selling the eagle as we crossed Wappoo Creek and turned on Maybank Highway on our way to the second store Saul had mentioned.

"Well, that was unproductive," Charles said.

"Unless you want to buy a hand-carved eagle," I said as I pulled in a small parking lot in front of a two-story building with plate-glass windows across the front. It could have been a furniture store in earlier times. Today the large sign over the door indicated it was the home of *Arnold's Antique Barn. Where the past will bring a smile to you today.*

Charles looked at the sign and mumbled, "The only thing that will bring a smile to me today is if Baby Jesus is in there."

I opened the oversized front door and was struck by the smell of mold and mildew rather than furniture polish.

As was the case in Harold Lee's store, we were the only customers and were greeted by a man who was ten years older than Charles and me. He wasn't as cheery as the last dealer and looked like he'd be more comfortable selling caskets. He wore a black suit that'd been worn so often the lining was visible at his elbows. It could be an antique. The man's smile was somber, but hard to focus on because of his distracting comb over.

"Gentlemen," he said by way of greeting and proof he didn't know us. "May I be of assistance?"

We introduced ourselves, and he said he was Arnold Tunny. We gave the same fictional account for our visit we had shared with Harold. Arnold listened and gave a somber nod like he was racking his brain to identify something we couldn't live without.

"Your collection sounds interesting," he said. "I admire anyone who appreciates the quality of inherited items and finds it in his or her heart to add to the collection. And, antique wooden items from Germany are held at a premium. Were there any particular items you were seeking?"

You bet there is, I thought, but said, "My grandmother had a fondness for religious icons, cherubs, angels, even animals. Anything along those lines would interest us."

"What price point were you looking for?"

It was a question I hadn't anticipated and off the top of my head said, "Four hundred tops."

"Oh."

It may have been my imagination, but it appeared his smile, as weak as it had been to start, had now weakened more.

"Where did you say you were from?" he added.

I hadn't, but told him Folly Beach.

"I hear it's interesting, although I prefer Isle of Palms. Neither here nor there. To answer your question, I don't believe I have anything that would meet your criteria. If you could leave your contact information, I will be glad to notify you if I come across something in which you might have an interest."

We thanked him for his time, avoided his request for our contact information, and pulled out of the parking lot.

"Another wasted stop," Charles said. "Not even an eagle."

"I'm not sure."

"Huh?"

"A couple of things bothered me." I turned on Folly Road and slammed on the brakes to avoid hitting a pick-up truck that had pulled in front of us. We skidded to a stop and glared at the man in the truck.

Charles braced himself on the dash. "Do I get to hear them?"

"Soon as I keep us from getting killed."

"I'll wait."

No vehicle body parts were exchanged, and we continued.

"First," I said, "he lost interest as soon as I said we had only a limited amount to spend."

"So," Charles said. "Maybe he only sells high-end stuff."

"Don't think so. The price tags on a few of the items near the front door were less than three hundred dollars, a couple less than a hundred. Besides, if he knew he didn't have the kind of German items we were asking about, why didn't he say it at first, rather than asking how much we were willing to pay."

Charles tapped on the console. "So you think he had the Baby Jesus, and either has a buyer who would pay more than you said, or knew it was worth more and didn't want to sell it to us?"

"That was my first thought."

Charles held up two fingers. "You said two things."

"Didn't you think it strange he asked where we were from?"

"Didn't think about it."

"I can see him asking, but at the beginning of our conversation. Clerks ask if they don't know the customer and want to have something to get them talking, but he asked after we told our story and he told us he didn't have anything. It struck me as odd."

"It's the kind of thing he might ask if he had the statue and knew where it had come from and was suspicious of why we were there."

I nodded. "I could be paranoid, but yes."

"Should we stop at Pewter Hardware and buy a crowbar and go back tonight and break in Arnold's and grab the statue?"

I hoped he was teasing, but at this point, I didn't have a better idea.

"Don't think so."

"How are we going to find out if he has it?"

I asked Charles to punch Chief LaMond's number in my phone and hand it to me.

Cindy said, "What are you pestering me about now?"

I continued to bemoan the fact the words *hi* and *hello* were dropped from the vocabulary. "A pleasant morning, chief."

"Yeah, yeah. What?"

"Have you heard from the detective who was on vacation?"

"No, why?"

"I wanted to ask him about a certain antique dealer who might not be on the up and up."

"Meddling again?"

"Asking questions."

"Chris, if it wasn't so close to Christmas, and I knew the big guy at the North Pole and the other one in Heaven weren't watching to see if I've been naughty or nice, I'd lay a string of profanities on you and tell you you're going to be the death of me yet. Instead, I'll tell you to butt out, and you'll say you will, and you won't. Crap, excuse me big guys, never mind. I'll call and see if they can track him down."

"You're an angel," I said.

"Of course, I am." The line went dead.

"No luck?" Charles said. "Why don't you call Karen? She could ask around to see if anyone knows anything about Arnold."

Karen worked major crimes and had been a detective with the Charleston County Sheriff's Office for several years. She was aware of my tendency to get involved in things I had no business getting involved with. When we had started dating she tolerated my involvement, but lately she had become increasingly irritated when she found out about my adventures. I didn't blame her.

"She's been tied up with a couple of murders and has been working around the clock. I don't want to bother her."

He looked at me like I had just fed him a crock, but un-Charles like, he let it go. I pulled in his parking lot. "I'll call you when I figure out how to get Jesus back," he said, and got out of the car.

"Short of crowbarring his door?"

"Maybe."

CHAPTER 17

Samuel and Jason stared at me from my front step as I pulled in the drive. They were wrapped in their high school jackets, and shivering like they had spent the day on an iceberg.

"Mr. Landrum." Samuel hopped up and jogged to the car door. "We thought you were never coming home."

"How long have you been here?"

Samuel looked at Jason, who said, "Hour or so. Figured you couldn't be gone too long."

"We were sort of wrong," Samuel said.

"Let's get in where it's warm," I headed to the door and noticed a box on the step. It was the size of a shoebox and had the Amazon logo on the side. The top was ripped, and there were cyan-colored stains on the bottom.

I motioned them in, and Jason picked up the box and followed me. I asked if they wanted anything to drink, and Samuel asked if I had hot chocolate. I said no, and they settled for a Pepsi. They followed me into the kitchen and after I had handed them their drinks, Samuel held the box in front of him like he was holding a gold bar.

"Mr. Landrum, we found the stolen package. It's not the valuable stuff, it's ink. It was already torn open when we found it. We didn't do it, honest."

116

He handed me the container.

"Where was it?"

Samuel rubbed his hands together to warm them. "Sort of in a big ole' trash dumpster behind Planet Follywood."

"Why were you looking in a dumpster?"

Samuel started to say something but hesitated and turned to Jason, who said, "We figured the cops were looking all over town and didn't think they'd want to get their hands dirty and stinky from looking in the trash. We've been looking where people throw stuff away. Thought the thief may get scared with all the cops running around trying to catch him and would dump the statue. We didn't find Jesus, but this was stolen too. It's evidence so maybe the police can dust it for prints, or get DNA, or something."

"Fellas, other than the large dumpsters, have you been rooting around in trash containers around houses again?"

Samuel glanced at Jason and turned back to me. "Sort of."

I frowned. "Did it enter your mind the person who stole it could live in one of those houses and could have seen you digging through the trash? Do you know the trouble you could have gotten in?"

"But Mr. Landrum, we—"

I glared at my young friends. "I'm not finished, Jason. You know your mother blames me for what happened a few years ago, and now she thinks I've encouraged you to get involved in this mess. And Samuel, remember what happened last year when you came close to getting killed? Both of you are wonderful, and I admire your enthusiasm and desire to help, but you must leave it to the police. How many times do I have to say it?"

Jason bowed his head. Samuel held out the mangled box. "What about this? It's a clue."

I didn't think it was much of one. "I'll get it to Chief

LaMond. I'll tell her how great it was you found it and I'm sure she'll see if there are prints on it."

Jason looked up. "Thanks, Mr. Landrum."

Samuel said, "We heard a rumor a bunch of money was stolen from First Light. Is it true?"

I told them it was.

"Jason and I were talking before you got here. We want to help get money to replace what was taken."

"That's kind."

Samuel smiled. "Yeah, we thought we could ride our bikes up Folly Road and rob a bank and give the money to Preacher Burl."

"He's teasing, Mr. Landrum," Jason added. "We were saying instead of giving each other Christmas gifts we could take what we already got back to the store and give the money we got for them to the preacher. Think it'd be okay?"

I was touched. I smiled and said, "It's a wonderful idea."

Samuel said, "We'd get more from the bank."

Jason smacked him on the arm.

***

A week ago, I'd told Charles I would take him Christmas shopping in Charleston. He hadn't gotten Heather anything and said he could use my help in selecting the "perfect" gift. I didn't know what I was getting Karen so I doubted I would be the person to find a perfect gift and told him so. He said it was true, but he needed someone to drive. It reminded me of why Rudolph was selected to lead Santa's sleigh. He had a shiny nose, and I had a car. With everything going on, I had forgotten Charles's request until the boys told me about getting gifts, or, not getting gifts.

I called and reminded Charles of our task, and he asked why I didn't think of it this morning when we were in downtown Charleston. I pleaded a senior moment, and he agreed—way too quickly. A half-hour later, I had dropped the torn box at the police station and Charles and I were back in the car. We took a slight detour and cruised past First Light's Nativity. Dude's employee Stephon was sitting on a bench in the Folly River Park across from the scene with his coat pulled tight around his trim body and a pea hat covering his ears. I waved at the sentinel and he gave a feeble half-wave in return.

Charles looked at Stephon and across the street at the display. "Closing the gate after the horse has skedaddled."

I headed to Charleston and listened to Bing Crosby singing "White Christmas" on satellite radio. The sun was shining, and the temperatures were mild, and for a moment, I thought about my childhood and how much fun it had been to see snow on the ground a few days before Christmas. I also recalled I was too young to drive, and the snow was more fun with dad behind the wheel.

"What are you getting Heather?"

"That's why you're along," Charles said.

"I thought it was to drive."

"The Christmas Song" played in the background. "That too."

"How about a carved eagle?"

"Too big," he said with a straight face.

"How about a car so I wouldn't have to drive you everywhere?"

"Wouldn't fit under the tree. I was thinking jewelry she could wear when she's performing."

"I like the car idea better, although jewelry would work."

Charles tilted his Tilley down over his eyes and said, "To the Market, James."

We parked in a surface pay lot at the east end of the historic Charleston City Market, and Charles, the master trivia collector, reminded me it was one of the oldest public markets in the country. He said there were more than three hundred vendors, and products ranging from pralines to purses, so he was certain he could find something for Heather. Karen was harder to shop for, and I had put off thinking about it until the last minute—not many minutes away.

A volunteer bell ringer manning a Salvation Army red kettle greeted us with "Merry Christmas" and a hopeful look as we crossed the street to the market's entry. Charles returned the greeting, and we dropped money in the kettle. We entered the crowded market, and I began thinking about someone's comment in the last few days about the "forgotten folks," the homeless who, for whatever reason, hadn't taken advantage of the charitable organizations, which provide services for the needy year-round, but more this time of year. I wondered how many of those people that organizations like the Salvation Army either are unable to assist or don't know about. Who had been talking about the forgotten folks?

Charles interrupted my thoughts when he held up a silver chain with an onyx palmetto tree dangling from it. "The perfect gift?"

"Nice," I said, not thinking it would qualify for the perfect gift category.

He shrugged, "Not Heather, is it?"

"Let's keep looking," I nudged him further down the aisle.

We stopped twice to sample the benne wafers and once for Charles to drool over, and exchange kisses with, a black and white Newfie the size of a Mini Cooper. We were blocking foot traffic, and I managed to separate man from dog. We weren't halfway through the market when Charles reminded me we hadn't eaten. I suggested the benne wafers were lunch and he suggested I was wrong, and pointed across the street and said he thought he heard Bubba Gump calling. I doubted it, but took the hint, and we walked over to Bubba Gump Shrimp Company and were seated at a table near the front of the chain restaurant.

"Shopping makes me hungry," Charles said as he scanned the menu. A waitress was quick to the table, and we each ordered a fish sandwich, a Dixie Fishwish in Gumpspeak, and Charles told the waitress he needed a beer because this was his busiest shopping day of the year. He was serious. I told her I needed wine because I was putting up with Charles. She headed to the kitchen and mumbled something that sounded a lot like, "Old farts."

"What are you getting Karen?"

"I hope I'll figure it out by the time we reach the end of the Market."

Charles looked out the front window where strands of colorful Christmas lights could be seen strung along the Market's roofline. "Did I ever tell you what Christmas meant when I was growing up?"

He had never told me much about his childhood except the basics about his parents dying when he was young and being raised by his grandmother. "Not much."

He continued to stare out the window. "I was eight or nine and all I wanted for Christmas was a bicycle. I was the only kid on the block who had to run beside my friends while they were riding bikes. All that running kept me in shape, but it was embarrassing. Each Christmas it seemed like one of my buddies got a shiny two-wheeler."

Our drinks arrived, and Charles took a long draw of beer.

"What happened?"

"To make sure granny got the message to Santa, I wrote her a note and printed *BICYCLE* in big red letters so if the jolly old man didn't have his glasses on, he could still read it. Even wrote a reminder note and gave it to her Christmas Eve."

"I'm thinking you didn't get a bike."

"I got up Christmas morning, put on my tennis shoes so I could ride the bike out the front door, scampered down the steps, and couldn't find anything with two wheels on it—

not under the tree, not in the kitchen, even looked outside. Being a selfish little brat, I decided it was the worst Christmas ever."

"I'm sorry."

Charles smiled. "I'm not. Know what I got?"

"A Corvette?"

Charles rolled his eyes but continued to smile. "Granny gave me a first edition of Agatha Christie's *The Hollow*."

I figured it must have been something special. "Wow."

"I didn't know what to make of it. Never heard of it. Granny explained it was a popular mystery written five years after I was born. She, being a librarian, was an expert on things bookish. She said the story was a great example of a 'country house mystery,' and she didn't think I would be interested in Tolstoy, Joyce, Eliot, or a bunch of other writers I'd never heard of. She thought a mystery might pique my interest in reading." He chuckled. "She said she'd paid $2.50 for it, and I'd better treat it like it was priceless."

"Did you ever get the bike?"

Food came before he answered. The sound system was playing "The Chipmunk Song," and Charles stuffed a fry in his mouth.

"Not for a few more years," he mumbled. "Know what I did get?"

I shook my head.

"An appreciation for books. Something about *The Hollow* grabbed me; hasn't let go yet. It was the first mystery I read. Didn't understand much of the British stuff in it, but something about it was exhilarating. Think it's why I tend to stick my nose in when someone gets killed over here. Anyway, for the next three years, she gave me a first edition of a popular novel. The next one was James A. Michener's *Tales of the South Pacific*. My favorites were mysteries. Reading grew on me."

"It explains the library in your apartment," I said, and thought the trauma of him not receiving a bike was why Charles's most prized possession to this day was his pristine 1961 Schwinn.

"Granny wasn't a barrel of laughs and seemed to always be wearing her scrunched up, librarian's face, but she taught me a lot about serious stuff. There was an old Bible in the house, and after I got hooked on reading, I read it from crinkly cover to cover. Like the British mysteries, I didn't understand a lot of it, although I got the strong feeling it wanted me to be a better person than I thought I could be. It made me not want to hurt anyone and be nice to everyone. I'm not always good at it, but I keep trying."

Charles was one of the nicest, although strangest, people I'd ever met. If it can be attributed to his stern grandmother or the Bible, I was thankful. Chuck Berry was rocking through the sound system with "Run Rudolph Run," and our plates were empty.

Charles pulled on his lightweight red jacket. "Let's get this shopping done."

The Market was more crowded than when we broke for lunch, so we spent more time avoiding running into people or being run over than we did shopping, but Charles found the perfect gift, a necklace with a silver guitar charm. He said it would complement her normal stage attire of a wide-brim hat and bright-colored blouse.

Finding a gift for Karen proved to be more difficult, but twenty minutes later, I settled on a sweet grass basket. Fifty artists weaving baskets were spread throughout the Market, and there were hundreds of baskets to choose from, so the problem wasn't finding the baskets; selecting the right one was the challenge. I took the lazy way out and purchased one from the vendor with the fewest people blocking my way. We made it back to the car without stopping—actually not true, Charles managed to find two more dogs to converse with before I had the heater blowing full blast and we were weaving through the narrow streets on our way out of downtown.

We were tired after shopping and didn't say much most of the way home. I was listening to Roy Orbison singing "Pretty Paper," when Charles turned down the volume, and said, "I was thinking. Instead of you and me getting presents for each other, we could donate whatever we would've spent to Preacher Burl to help make up for what was stolen?"

I had already decided to reach into my savings and give the preacher whatever he needed. I thought it was touching that Charles had the idea.

"That's a great idea," I said, and told him Samuel and Jason were doing the same thing.

"Wonderful, some other people told me they were going to do that too. Nobody is going to get away with stealing the spirit of Christmas from Folly." He glanced over at me and smiled. "I think Preacher Burl will be able to use the lump of coal I was getting you."

"Ho, Ho, Ho," I said.

On the radio, Ray Stevens was singing "Santa Claus is Watching You."

CHAPTER 18

We had passed Harris Teeter when I spotted a familiar person walking along the road and struggling to carry three plastic grocery bags. I pulled over and waited for the man to get beside the car.

"Bernard," I said. "Hop in, we'll give you a ride."

He panted, and between labored breaths, said, "Don't mind if I do."

He put his groceries on the back seat and slipped in. He was more clean-shaven than the last time I'd seen him, but his hair looked like it hadn't made contact with a comb in days. He had on a heavy Carhartt jacket, a vast improvement over the tattered army coat he'd worn in Cal's.

Charles said, "Grocery shopping?"

He exhaled. "Yes, sir. Never been in there before. It sure is big."

"A long walk from Folly, too," Charles said, leaning on the obvious.

"Yep." Bernard chuckled. "My Rolls is in the shop."

Charles laughed. "Hate it when that happens. That a new coat? Looks good."

I couldn't see Bernard's reaction, but heard him wiggling around in the seat. "Thanks, sir. Hitched into town yesterday and got it. It's good and warm. Christmas season's been good to me."

"That's great," I said. New coat, first time to Harris Teeter, three bags of food. Curious.

"What made it so good? I could use some of that luck." Charles asked.

He had a knack for asking personal questions without raising the ire of the recipient.

"Umm, came into a bit of money. Got a question, any—"

Charles interrupted, "Where'd it come from?"

Charles wouldn't let go. If I was Bernard, I'd be flinging a banana from the grocery bag at him.

Bernard ignored Charles. "Ya'll heard if they caught the guy who stole Baby Jesus?"

I remembered how interested he'd appeared in the theft the first time we'd met.

"Not yet," I said. "Hear more rumors about who it might be?"

"One, sir. The early talk about witches seems to be bad intel. Surfers are still the word around town."

"Where'd you say the money came from?" Charles "Persistent" Fowler asked.

Bernard laughed. "Charles, I don't recall saying."

I thought, *Good for you, Bernard.*

Charles said, "Oh."

Bernard surprised me. "Might as well tell you. It was pretty exciting. I woke up the other morning and stepped out of my sleeping bag. Stumbled over a big ole rock in front of it and reached down to throw it away. Know what I found under the rock?"

Charles said, "A worm."

My admiration for the stranger increased when once again Bernard ignored Charles, and said, "Under the rock were six fifty-dollar bills. Not a soul around. It was like the bills crawled under the rock and were waiting for me to find them."

"Incredible," Charles said, and again asked, "Where'd it come from?"

"Can't say I've believed in Santa since—well, I don't know when. Yesterday morning all those visions of sugarplums dancing in my head rushed back. Nearly peed in my jeans, I was so excited."

Charles again said, "Where did—"

"I'm getting there. The funny thing is I don't know her."

Charles said, "Who?"

"The person who left the money, some woman named Tabatha."

"How do you know?" I asked.

"She left a note with the money. It said, *Merry Christmas from Tabatha.*"

I asked, "Still have the note?"

"No, sir. I stuck it in my pocket but it must have fallen out. I'll tell you one thing. Whoever she is, she sure made my Christmas."

Charles repeated, "Incredible," and threw out another question from the *none of your business* file, "Where are you staying?"

"Charles, you sure are a nosy one. Ain't anyone ever told you curiosity killed the cat?"

Three zillion times, I thought.

Charles laughed. "A time or two." It was one of the few times Charles understated something. "So where are you staying?"

"Nowhere in particular. You ain't going to tell the cops?"

"My lips are sealed," Charles said.

That would be a Christmas miracle, but instead of saying it, I kept *my* lips sealed.

"I've been spending nights under some of those elevated houses out past the dentist's office. Don't stay in one place too long. The cops frown on it if they start getting calls from people complaining about me hanging around."

"Ever stayed in one of those shelters over there," Charles asked and pointed toward Charleston.

"Used to, except some of those do-gooders who run them said I was prone to get in fights with their other guests. Told me not to come back."

Charles said, "That's too bad."

"Nah," Bernard said, "Didn't fancy being there anyway. Crazy people everywhere. Smelly. Danged drunks. Besides, the people in charge got it right about me. I have what you call a quick temper. Better being alone."

We were crossing the new bridge to Folly and I said, "Where do you want us to take you?"

"You can let me out anywhere. Won't be far to my mansion."

"Sure we can't take you closer?"

"Yes. I'll be fine anywhere, sir."

Clearly, Bernard didn't want us to know the location of his sleeping-bag mansion.

I pulled to the curb in front of the library and Charles turned to the back seat. "Don't forget Cal's invitation to his Christmas party. He's got a big day planned."

"I'll check my calendar," Bernard said. "While we're talking about Christmas stuff, think preacher, umm whatever his name is—"

"Preacher Burl Costello."

"Yeah, that's it. Think Preacher Burl would mind me dropping in on his Christmas Eve preaching?"

"He'd be pleased if you did," I said.

Bernard stepped out of the car, set his grocery bags on the sidewalk, and rubbed his mustache. "I'll try to be there. Will it be in the store?"

"The preacher is hoping for good weather so he can hold it on the beach," Charles said. "The storefront church may be too small to hold everyone."

"Reckon I can find it, fellas. Thanks for the lift."

128

We watched him walk in the direction of what I assumed to be the house he'd been staying under, and I pulled back in the line of traffic.

Elvis was singing his version of "Blue Christmas," Charles sang along with the last verse, and turned the radio's volume down. "Believe his story?"

"That Elvis'll have a blue Christmas?"

Teasing Charles was one of my true pleasures.

"Bernard?"

"I'd like to. It's heartwarming, a Hallmark moment. Money left for a homeless person a few days before Christmas. But, I have trouble with it. It sounds unrealistic, and remember the other night at Cal's?"

"I need more information."

"Cal was surprised when Bernard came in and had a couple of beers."

"No surprise there," Charles said. "Didn't he say Bernard had come in several times?"

"Yes, but the other times he never had money. Cal footed the bill."

"Yeah." Charles rubbed his chin. "He seemed interested if the cops had leads on the Baby Jesus thief."

"Like he did a few minutes ago."

"Think he stole everything?"

"I hate to say it, although I wouldn't be surprised. If he did, he'd have had to have access to a vehicle or someone helping him. I can't see him walking around lugging two surfboards or the statue."

We sat in his parking lot debating Bernard's guilt, and realized while we may think he was guilty, we couldn't prove it. Charles asked if I thought we should tell Chief LaMond. I said we didn't have anything concrete to tell her.

"Let me throw out another thought," I said.

"Throw away."

"Say he's telling the truth and he did get the money with a note. Who's Tabatha?"

Charles tilted his head my direction. "I don't know any Tabathas. Do you?"

"No."

"She pays better than the tooth fairy," Charles said as he got out of the car.

I pulled out of Charles's lot and realized that while I wasn't hungry, I knew I would have as good a chance finding something to eat at the house as I would finding a Tyrannosaurus Rex in my front yard. I parked and walked across Center Street to Planet Follywood. Food might help me think.

Planet Follywood was one of the town's most popular restaurants and hosted live entertainment weekend nights, karaoke every Thursday, and a wide selection of beach grub all the time. Tonight it also featured Mayor Brian Newman at a table near the jukebox. He was alone, had a serving of fried okra in front of him, and was sipping a Corona. Brian waved me over and asked if I wanted to join him. He was mayor, father of the woman I was dating, and an all-around good guy, so I couldn't see why not. Camille, one of the waitresses, was quick to the table and asked if I wanted Cabernet. I said yes, and wondered if it was bad that I was known at most restaurants in town by my drink preference.

The mayor was a handful of years older than me, but unlike me, he had spent thirty years in the military as an MP and in Special Services. Also unlike me, he was tall, trim, confident and though he had been out for years, oozed military. He had been Folly's police chief for twenty years before becoming mayor.

"What trouble have you been getting in today?" Brian asked.

"None."

"Not how I hear it."

I gave him my most innocent look. "What have you heard?"

"Rumor is you and your sidekick Charles have been asking around about our recent rash of thefts."

On Folly, rumors spread as quickly as norovirus on a cruise ship, so I wasn't surprised he'd heard. "We're worried about Preacher Burl and how the theft of Baby Jesus has affected him and First Light."

Camille returned with my wine and asked if I wanted anything to eat. I asked Brian if he was getting anything else; he said a chef salad with grilled chicken. I refrained from saying "yuck" to his healthy choices, and ordered a patty melt.

Brian said, "Chris, I'm not encouraging you to meddle in police business." He hesitated and chuckled. "History says I couldn't stop you if I tried, but I'm as frustrated over it as I've been about anything since I've been mayor. The theft of a little wooden carving has done more to suck the life of Christmas out of this tight-knit community than anything I can imagine. Do you know how many people have come to me asking if it's been found?" I figured it was rhetorical, shook my head, and waited for him to continue. "I tell them no and they, to a person, tell me how much seeing First Light's Nativity had meant to them, and how devastated they are by the theft. The Nativity scene at the Catholic Church has always meant a lot, but something about First Light having one touches so many, especially so many who wouldn't set foot in other churches."

"I'm sure Chief LaMond is doing everything possible."

A reggae song blared from the jukebox. Brian stared at the machine, at the Christmas tree sitting beside it, and at me. "I told her to do whatever she needed to do. Forget our overtime restrictions and find the statue." He nodded and smiled. "When I was a kid, my two brothers and I got to play the three wise men in a living Nativity our Sunday school had." Brian smiled. "We got dressed up like the wise men you see in most scenes. We set up in front of our church and the two Sundays before Christmas we stood out in the cold while people came to the morning worship service. We looked silly in our fake beards and all, but I was amazed how many people stood and looked at us like they were looking at the real thing. I can't explain it. It was wonderful— spiritual, you could say."

I nodded. "That's what I've heard people say about the Nativity at the Catholic Church and First Light's scene."

"It's why the mindless theft of that small statue has torn a hole out of the heart of so many people."

Our food arrived, Stevie Wonder's version of "What Christmas Means to Me" played on the jukebox, and Brian drifted into thought. I wondered if he was reliving those memorable Sundays.

Our conversation turned to more cheerful topics and he asked if I had seen Karen lately. He seemed surprised when I said it had been a couple of weeks, but understood considering her workload had increased during the holiday season. Good tidings and great joy, mixed with excessive amounts of liquid spirits, sometimes disintegrated into tension, anger, and murder. As Karen had often said, "When bad things happen, I go to work." She'd worked a lot this holiday season.

Our food was gone as were two bottles of beer and two glasses of wine. Brian thanked me for joining him and letting him share his wise man story and bemoan the effect the loss of the statue was having on his city. I told him it was always a pleasure to talk with him and headed home.

I had turned on the light when the phone rang.

"Dude be here."

"Chris be here."

"Intros be done. Message. Be having meeting of surfer crime stoppers."

"Surfers Against Spirit of Christmas Thieves."

"That's what me say."

Don't think so, I thought. "When and where?"

"Here. *Manana*. Two hours past sun disappearing."

"At the surf shop?"

He repeated, "That's what me say."

"Seven o'clock tomorrow?"

"You got it."

The phone went dead.

I stared at the phone, smiled, and figured he was inviting me to the meeting. That's what me say.

CHAPTER 19

I called Charles the next morning and extended an invitation to what I understood to be a meeting of the surfer group. He pouted and asked why I hadn't asked him last night. I said I waited until this morning to irritate him; he said I had succeeded. He then told me he'd meet me in front of the surf shop at six-thirty. I said I hoped he didn't freeze waiting for me that early.

True to his word, Charles was standing in front of the surf shop at six-thirty. Untrue to my word, I was there as well. He smiled and said he was glad I'd learned to tell time.

Dude, Finley, and Stephon were the only people in the shop. The rest of the surfer group didn't follow Charles Standard Time. Finley seemed surprised to see us, Stephon gave his normal reaction and snarled in our direction, and Dude said, "Aloha."

Dude picked up Pluto, who had been leaning against his leg, kissed the Australian Terrier on the mouth, and turned to Finley and Stephon. "They be special guests."

Finley seemed less than thrilled, but thanked us for coming while Stephon continued to snarl. The awkward moment was broken when three more members of the group arrived. I recognized Deb, and Truman, but didn't know the third person. Dude continued to hold Pluto and pointed at the newcomers with his free hand and said, "Be Deb, Truman, and Andy."

Charles and I nodded to the three. Deb smiled and said, "Uncle Saul told me you came to see him. He's a little stuffy, so I hope he was friendly. He told me he was uncomfortable talking about dealers, but did anyway since I had asked him to help. Did he help you figure out who stole Jesus?"

Truman, Andy, and Finley stopped talking and stared at Charles and me.

I said, "Afraid not."

"Boards and bling?" Dude asked.

Charles said, "Nope."

Dude tapped the floor with his florescent-green tennis shoe. "Bummer."

Four more surfers arrived, and Finley looked at his watch. "Let's start."

The newcomers ignored the rest of us and were in deep conversation about parking tickets. Finley raised his voice and repeated it was time to start. It took and everyone moved to the center of the room. The display racks hadn't been moved as much as they had been for the first meeting and we were crammed together.

Finley pushed his long, sun-bleached blond hair out of his eyes and pulled his shoulders back. "It's almost Christmas, so let's begin by singing a Christmas carol. I was thinking "Jingle Bell Rock.""

I wondered in what carol book he'd found "Jingle Bell Rock," but was impressed he was trying to honor the Christmas spirit. Finley raised his arms like a choir director, lowered them and we began singing. The group's effort was spirited, although it became clear the first seven words were the only words any of us knew in the "carol." After repeating them twice, Finley waved for us to stop. The phrase *it's the thought that counts* popped to mind.

Deb and Teddye laughed. Truman said, "Good job."

"Okay, enough," Finley said. "This is important. Christmas Day is around the corner and I wanted to get together and talk about anything new we know about the stealing. Has anybody called about the reward?" Finley looked around the room.

Dude set Pluto on the floor and said, "That be *grande* N-O."

Finley looked at Pluto who had run to Deb and whimpered for her to pick him up. She did and Finley said, "That's what I thought. We've been watching the Nativity ever since we met here. I haven't heard anything, but has anyone seen anybody suspicious, something you may not have thought important at the time?"

Andy, the surfer I hadn't seen before, said, "Don't know how important it is. Two kids keep riding by. Saw them three or four days."

"Yeah," Teddye said. "They never stopped while I was watching. I saw them ride past a few times."

"Finley," I said. "That's Jason and Samuel. They're a couple of high school kids who are concerned about the thefts. The other day, they found one of the stolen packages and turned it over to the police. They're okay."

Deb said, "The jewelry?"

"The ink cartridges."

Stephon said, "A big whoop."

Deb said, "May not have been Jesus, the boards, or the jewels, but it's better than we've done."

Finley waited for Deb to finish. "Good, it explains the kids. Anybody see anything else suspicious?"

"A bunch of old folks sitting across from the Nativity in geezer cars, Buicks and Mercurys." Truman said. "Half the time they were asleep. They couldn't catch a cold on a germ farm."

Finley shook his head. "Truman, you know they're from the churches doing the same thing we are by keeping watch over the Nativity. We should appreciate them." He turned away from Truman. "What about you guys?" He stared at Charles and me. "You're the bad guy catchers. Who did it?"

I looked at Finley and at the others. "I wish we knew. What I will tell you is we're not done."

Finley shook his head and looked at the group. "Anything else?"

Andy said, "Yeah, well maybe." He hesitated and looked around. "A man who lives in my building lost his job a couple of months ago. He has some strange disease and kept missing work. He didn't want anybody at work to know about his illness and didn't tell his boss what was wrong. They fired him. He's squeaking by and about to lose the apartment. I've seen him going through the trash along the street trying to find something to hock or to eat. Poor guy. He'd told me he didn't want to get any help from the groups, which help people like him. Too much pride, and—"

Stephon interrupted. "What's your point?"

Andy glared at Stephon and turned to Finley. "I ran into him yesterday. He was getting out of his rusted-out Chevy pick-up truck. He had on a new winter coat. The tag was still sewn on the sleeve, but I didn't want to embarrass him by saying anything. I said, 'Nice coat.' His face turned red, and he mumbled thanks. I noticed he had spanking new tires on his truck. They stood out like an army tank rollin' down Center Street. He saw me looking at them and said, 'You won't believe what happened.'" Andy paused.

Paused too long for Charles. "What?"

Andy said, "Now I'm reporting what he said, you understand? He went into this unbelievable story. Said he came out of his apartment the day before yesterday and there was an envelope taped to his door. Guess what he said was in it?" No one guessed, so Andy continued, "Ten, fifty-dollar bills—yep, five hundred bucks stuck on his door."

"Sure there were," Stephon said and rolled his eyes.

Finley asked, "Who were they from?"

"Claims he didn't know. Can you believe it?"

"Wow," said Truman. "It's great, since he wouldn't ask for help from anyone. It's nice somebody wanted to help. I wonder how many more people around here can't get help when they need it? I think I know who you're talking about. Isn't it—"

Andy waved his hand in Truman's face. "We shouldn't say his name."

Truman started to say something, but hesitated. "Okay."

"You think he's lying and he's the person who took the baby and the other stuff?" Deb asked.

Andy said, "I don't want to say that. I feel sorry for the man. He seems like a nice guy, but doesn't it sound fishy? Someone stuck money on his door and he doesn't know who."

Stephon said, "I think he's the thief."

I thought of Bernard's windfall and the note from Tabatha. "Was there a note with his money?"

Andy seemed surprised I had spoken. "He didn't mention one. He was all excited about the cash. Why?"

"Curious," I said. "If you would, ask him the next time you see him."

"Okay, I guess."

A couple of the other surfers started talking.

I stepped close to Finley and looked at the group. "I don't know if the man you're talking about stole the statue, or for that matter, stole anything." I pointed at Andy. "You need to tell the police, and if there was a note, please let me know." He wrote my number on his palm and said he would.

"What have the cops done so far?" Stephon grumbled. "Why do you think they'll do anything?"

Charles, who had been silent, stepped beside me. "Chris and I know Chief LaMond better than any of you know her. She's as concerned about finding the statue as you

138

are. I'd trust her with my life and Chris is right. You need to talk to her."

Andy looked for support from his fellow surfers and turned to Charles. "Okay, but it won't do any good."

Dude took three steps and took Pluto from Deb's arms and pointed a finger at Andy. "You be seein' chieftress."

Andy nodded.

"Soon," Dude said.

Andy nodded a second time.

Finley asked if there was anything else to be shared and when no one answered he asked if we wanted to end the meeting with another Christmas song.

Unlike the group's rendition of "Jingle Bell Rock," "No!" was shouted in perfect harmony.

Each of the surfers patted Pluto's head before heading out, most to local bars to get more in the holiday spirit. Charles and I stood on the sidewalk.

Charles looked up the steps to the door of Dude's shop. "The five hundred dollars stuck on the door sounds like another story we heard."

"Bernard's three hundred dollars under a rock."

"Yep. It's why you asked about a note."

"Both men down on their luck," I said. "Both, for whatever reason, unable or unwilling to get assistance."

"If they're telling the truth, it seems we have a secret Santa handing out big bucks."

"Secret Santa named Tabatha. I still see more questions than answers. Are Andy's neighbor and Bernard telling the truth? If they are, is there a connection between the thefts and the gifts? If so, why would someone commit crimes and give the money away?"

Charles said. "I think the person who stole the stuff is doing it. It's Robin Hood in our hood." He pulled his jacket closed. "Tell you what else I know. I'm freezing my keister off. Let's figure this out tomorrow."

CHAPTER 20

I had a hard time sleeping. I tossed, turned, and replayed the meeting in my head. Christmas Eve was two days away, and it didn't seem I was closer to honoring Burl's request to find Baby Jesus than I was the morning I had learned it was missing. What I did know was the theft of the statue wasn't a prank, and the surfer group, the church members, and the police were doing what they could to find it. Since the surfer meeting had ended, something was tickling the far reaches of my memory, something important. But what? It was tied to the surfer meeting, or something said at the meeting that reminded me of something else. The only thing that struck me as important was Andy's neighbor finding the money, if, in fact, he had. Did the neighbor have anything in common with Bernard, the alleged recipient of another gift? There was no doubt both were down on their luck, although so were many others. Is Tabatha the link?

What else did I know about the missing items? Chief LaMond assured me she was working with the police in Charleston to check the city's pawnshops to see if the jewelry showed up, but I wasn't optimistic. Years ago, Brian Newman had told me pawn shops were good about recordkeeping and identifying people who left items with them, but no shortage of other less-savory individuals would buy and fence items. The no-questions-asked crowd could have purchased the jewelry, and the police wouldn't have a way to trace it.

What about the statue? I thought about Charles and my conversation with Deb's uncle and the antique dealers he'd referred us to. What was it that bothered me about the last dealer we talked to? Oh yeah, Arnold at Arnold's Antique Barn, and how we'd told him we were looking for German antiques and he didn't say he didn't have any until we told him how much we wanted to spend, and how unusual it was when he asked us where we were from. When we said Folly, he rushed us out of the store. It was as if he knew what we were looking for. Granted, there was nothing in what he had said that could implicate him, but it felt off.

There was still something bothering me from the meeting in the surf shop.

Sleep must have come, because the next thing I remembered was waking up, glancing out the window, and seeing daylight. What I didn't see was an answer to what had bothered me.

***

I was headed to Bert's for coffee when I saw Mary Ewing leaving the store. She had a paper bag in one hand and held her two-year-old's hand with the other. Her older girl was on the other side of the young one and was holding her hand as they crossed the street and headed toward the beach. Three cars stopped for them to cross.

There were half dozen customers in the store. Three were standing at the coffee urn in back, two were fawning over a Lab near the beer coolers, and, Lisa, the clerk, was adjusting the volume on an old-fashioned boom box behind the counter. It was playing "Little Drummer Boy."

I waited for one of Bert's regulars to put sugar in his

coffee, and I drew a cup. Lisa had finished with the boom box and waved at me. "Merry almost Christmas."

I smiled and thanked her. She asked if I was doing anything special for the holiday, and I said I was going to First Light's Christmas Eve service and planned to be at Cal's Christmas Day. She said she had to work Christmas Eve but was off Christmas and would try to "meander over to Cal's." She asked if Karen was coming and I said I didn't know.

"I know what you mean," Lisa said. "Seems killings are almost as common around Christmastime as sales at the mall."

I looked at the door. "Lisa, what do you know about the lady and the two kids who just left?"

"Mary, Jewel, and Joanie?"

I wasn't surprised Lisa knew their names. "Yes."

"Don't know a lot. They come in a couple of times a week. Jewel's six and Joanie's two. Mary usually buys milk and packaged food. She pays with a handful of change; counts it out like it's precious diamonds." Lisa hesitated and lowered her voice. "She doesn't always have enough. We kick in the difference. It's only a dollar or two. Figure most of the food's for the kids."

"Know where she lives?"

Lisa shook her head. "She doesn't say much, sort of shy, I think. I don't like to ask many questions. Ever once and a while, when she has a few extra dollars, she hires one of our young clerks to babysit for a few hours. Mary takes the kids to the sitter's apartment so the sitter doesn't know where they live. Why?"

"Curious. I met her with a couple of surfers at Cal's the other night."

Two more customers entered and Lisa said she'd better get to work. I thanked her, paid and grabbed my coffee. "Have a Merry Little Christmas" was playing in the background. From the way things were going, I began to doubt I would.

Instead of going home, I zipped my jacket, pulled my Tilley down low on my head, and headed in the direction Mary had gone. The temperature was mild although the breeze off the ocean was chilling, and the sky was clear and the bright sunshine tempered the chill, but only a little.

I crossed East Arctic Avenue, looked each way, but didn't see Mary. I reached the wooden walkway that crossed over the dunes line separating the small parking area from the beach, and saw Mary sitting on the other side. A child was on each side of her, huddled close to their mother, and eating powdered mini-donuts. Mary had coffee in one hand and a plastic orange juice container in the other. She also had on what appeared to be a new, mid-length cloth coat.

I pretended to be surprised to see them and Mary looked at me like she recognized me from somewhere but didn't know where. I told her we had met in Cal's and at church. She smiled and apologized for not recognizing me, and said she had been distracted. The kids looked over their shoulder at me and smiled. Each had on new clothes.

Mary pulled one of the children closer so I could pass. I did and pointed to the oldest child's fire engine red, mud boots. "Pretty boots."

She gave a wide smile and Mary turned to her. "Jewel, thank the nice man."

"Thank you," Jewel said, much more polite than most of my friends would have been. "They're new." She stood and pirouetted. "So's my coat and dress."

"They're lovely," I said and returned her smile.

Joanie looked at her mom and raised her hand. Mary put her arm around her and said, "Joanie's boots, coat, and dress are new too." Joanie tried to pirouette like Jewel had and tripped and landed on the ramp. Jewel giggled, and fortunately, so did Joanie.

Mary pulled the girls close. "We don't live far from here, but the girls don't get to see the ocean often."

I kneeled and looked at the little girls. Powdered sugar was sprinkled on the front of their coats. "The ocean's neat, isn't it?"

Jewel answered. "It sure is. Momma said she's going to bring us here every day until Christmas and even on Christmas Day. She got us these new clothes, but said seeing the ocean is our Christmas present. She said kids everywhere could get clothes, but only special ones could see the ocean for real and not just in books or on TV."

"Your mom's a smart lady."

Jewel nodded. "Me, too."

I smiled. "You sure are."

Joanie raised her hand again, and I patted her on the knee. "You are, too."

Mary slid over to the edge of the ramp. "I'm being rude. Would you like to sit?"

I wouldn't have wanted to interfere with her kids Christmas present, but was curious about where she could have gotten the money for new clothes, after what Lisa had said about Mary not having money for food.

"If you don't mind."

Jewel patted the space beside her.

A woman with two boys about the girls' ages approached us as they walked down the beach. They were following two German shepherds.

"Mom," Jewel said. "Can we pet the dogs?"

"You don't know them," Mary said. "I don't think—"

Joanie squealed, "Pleeeze."

The woman with the dogs looked over and smiled. "They're friendly."

Mary sighed, shook her head. "Okay, but don't pester the sweet lady, and be sure to thank her when you're done."

Jewel and Joanie were halfway to the dogs before Mary could caution them to be careful.

"Great kids," I said.

Mary continued to watch the girls. "I'm blessed to

have them."

The kids stood on each side of one of the dogs and hugged it like it was a long-lost relative.

I continued to watch the dog and the kids. "You live here long?"

She glanced over at me. "No. Just since...." She paused and looked at the pier.

"Since what?" I asked, and hoped I wasn't being too nosy.

She looked down at the sand on the step and up at me. "I had a job at a convenient store in Charleston after my husband, umm, was gone, but got laid off because of some tax trouble the owners got in. We didn't have anywhere over there to live, and I got to know some guys here and moved."

"What happened to your husband?"

She again looked down at the sand.

I was afraid my Charles-like questioning had gone too far, and I didn't say anything. The German shepherds were sitting in the sand, and the girls were running around them with the boys.

The wind was picking up, and Mary whispered, "He's in prison."

"I'm sorry."

She pointed to her girls. "I'm not. He gave me Joanie, the greatest gift possible."

"She's a doll."

"Yes," Mary hesitated before saying, "My husband was selling drugs, and I didn't know a danged thing about it. I felt so stupid."

"Will he be away long?"

She glanced at the girls, and said, "He was caught in the back of a warehouse selling to an undercover cop. Instead of giving up, the idiot tried to shoot his way out." She shook her head. "He shot a police officer. Thank God it didn't kill him. I don't know when he'll ever get out. I hope he doesn't. I don't want him to see Joanie, and I don't want her to see him again—never again.”

She looked back at the sand and a tear rolled down her cheek. I wanted to put my arm around her, but didn’t. Laughter from the four kids and a couple of barks from the dogs were the only sounds I heard.

Mary looked up at the kids. “I’m so ashamed. I can’t bear to go to a homeless shelter because the people there always want to hear what happened. I can’t tell them.”

“I’m sure they’ve heard worse, Mary. It wasn’t your fault.”

She looked at the girls and yelled, “Jewel, Joanie, come on back now and let the nice lady get on with her walk.”

Joanie dropped her head. “Mom.”

“It’s fine,” the lady with the dogs said. “The dogs need a rest anyway. They’re okay.”

I smiled at Mary. “You’re outnumbered.”

She wiped the tear from her cheek. “It’s nice to see them happy. Doesn’t happen too much. Hope her next few years aren’t as rough as poor Jewel’s.”

I wondered how to ask what she’d meant without being pushy and regressed to what I’d learned in college psychology. “Oh.”

I was afraid my rusty technique had failed until she said, “I grew up near Chicago and never finished high school.” She hesitated. “Don’t know why I’m telling you this; don’t even know you.”

“Sometimes it’s easier to tell a stranger than it is to tell someone you know.”

“I guess. I was in the tenth grade and started dating.” She air quoted, ‘the greatest guy in the world.’” She looked down at the sand. “I got pregnant and learned the second I told him he wasn’t so great.”

“He dumped you?”

She chuckled. “Quick as a hummingbird.”

“Sorry.”

"If you can believe it, that wasn't the worst of it. My parents wanted me to get rid of the baby, wanted me to get an abortion. They insisted. I wasn't the brightest kid around, after all, I was pregnant and in the tenth grade, but I couldn't see how it was the right thing to do. I told mom I wasn't going to." She stopped and looked back at the sand.

"What happened?"

She looked up and pointed to her children. "Jewel."

I patted her arm. "Perfect name."

She nodded. "They didn't kick me out of the house, but I felt unwanted. I took some of my things and the little money I had saved from babysitting and bought a bus ticket to Birmingham, Alabama."

"Why Birmingham?"

She smiled. "Have you ever been in Chicago in January?"

I shook my head.

"I figured I had to go south where it was warmer, and I didn't have enough money to get to Florida, so Birmingham was it. Found a shelter for the homeless that had a special area for kids like me. They helped me get a job at a convenient food store. Jewel was born and was the prettiest baby I'd ever seen."

I smiled. "She still is."

"Thank you. You're mighty easy to talk to."

"Sometimes it helps to talk."

"Wanna know about Joanie?"

"Only if you want to tell me."

"I met her dad in Birmingham. Vernon's his name. It was three years ago, around Christmas, in fact. He came in the store, and I thought he was the cutest guy I'd seen since I was there. He was a charmer. Kept coming in and buying chewing gum and he finally asked me out. Dumb me, I said yes. Well, to make a long story short, he proposed on our third date and we got married at the courthouse two weeks later." She smiled. "I was married when I got pregnant with

Joanie." Her smile faded. "I thought everything was going fine. He had a job and brought in a pretty good amount of money. Honest, Mr. Landrum, I had no idea he was getting it selling drugs."

"I believe you."

"Thank you. And then the drug bust and that's when he shot the policeman. Oh God, I was so ashamed. I had to get away and with Jewel in one hand and a child carrier with Joanie in it in the other hand, I got on another Greyhound and ended up in Charleston." She looked over at me. "So there's my story. Hope I haven't got you all depressed about it."

I smiled and patted her arm. "All I see is a sweet young lady with two wonderful children who are spending time with their mom, playing with two big dogs, and being thrilled to have the gift of the ocean for Christmas."

She patted my hand. "I am blessed. This may be the best Christmas I've had in forever. You know what happened?"

"What?"

She pointed to her two girls. "All the new clothes, a couple more surprise gifts I'll be giving them Christmas morning, because of a gift from someone I don't know."

"Gift?"

"Two days ago there was an envelope under the door of the house...umm, the house where I'm staying. I still can't believe it, there were six, hundred dollar bills in it. At first, I thought it was a mistake, but since the house was supposed to be, umm, vacant, it had to be for me, didn't it?"

"Seems like it," I said, and thought of the money Bernard and the man in the apartment had received.

"I probably should have turned it over to the police, but what would I say? Besides, Christmas was a few days away and I wanted to take the girls to church Christmas Eve and thought how wonderful it would be if they didn't have to wear tattered clothes. Maybe us having a few days without looking poor would be good. What should I have done?"

"Do you have any idea who left it?"

She looked down at the sand and mumbled, "There was a note."

Bernard all over again, I thought. "Did it say *Merry Christmas from Tabatha?*"

She jerked her head up. "How did you know?"

I started to answer, when she said, "Did you say Tabatha?"

I nodded.

"No, it was from someone named Tiffany."

"Are you sure?"

"Yes," she said and smiled. "It reminded me of that fancy jewelry store."

Could Bernard have gotten the name wrong? Could his note have said Tiffany? If it did, it was far beyond a coincidence some of the jewelry stolen was from Tiffany and now money was being left with a note from Tiffany. Charles was right. There was a connection between the thefts and the gifts.

Mary interrupted my thoughts. "Mr. Landrum, are you okay?"

"Oh, sorry Mary. My mind was wandering. Umm, who knew where you were staying?"

"You're not going to get me in trouble, are you?"

"No."

"A few people know, I guess. People who live nearby see us coming and going. I don't think I've told anyone in town. I wanted to tell the nice folks at Bert's because they help me sometimes, but I didn't."

I remembered a light on next door to Finley's house the night Charles and I were there. Finley had said the house was a rental, and squatters occasionally found their way in. "Mary, are you staying in a house on East Eric?"

She stared at me. "Why did you say that?"

"A few nights ago I was at Finley Livers' house and—"

Mary shook her head and interrupted, "He said he wouldn't tell."

I guess that was yes. "He didn't tell me." I explained about seeing the light on and what he had said about squatters.

"It's us. Finley even gave me a ride to Wal-Mart to buy the clothes for the girls. He said we could stay at his house but he'd already rented out the upstairs. Said if the guys living there ever moved, we could have it, real cheap. He's a nice guy."

"You know you can't stay where you are long. It's a rental, and you never know when it'll be needed."

"Mr. Landrum, I know, but I don't know what to do."

"May I make a suggestion?"

"Sure."

"Preacher Burl is a good friend. He understands the bad situations people can get in, and best of all, he's not judgmental. He cares and has helped many people find housing, find jobs, and find their way through rough times. I'd suggest you talk to him, lay everything out, and trust him. He can help."

She tilted her head. "Do you think so?"

"I know so."

"Funny you say that about him. I haven't been to church for a while, umm, years, but when I heard people talking about the Christmas Eve service, something told me I should go. It's why I asked him if children were invited. I liked the way he said yes. He didn't even think about it. It's why I was so happy to get new clothes for my girls."

"He'd love to see you there tomorrow night."

The woman was calling the dogs to continue their walk. Jewel and Joanie hugged the dogs bye, and Mary hugged me.

CHAPTER 21

On the way home, I kept thinking even though the spirit of Christmas may have been sucked out of the hearts of some because of the missing statue, how Mary, despite what many would consider to be a tragic young life, was making the most of the season. She was sharing the ocean with her children and told them how lucky they were to see it firsthand. She had taken the mysterious gift and bought clothes for her children so they would look their best at church Christmas Eve. Mary was a survivor, a survivor who had valued life enough to stand up to her parents at a huge cost and had given birth to Jewel. Yes, Mary was a survivor who had stood strong when many would have given up.

I walked in the door and felt the blast of heat from the overworked furnace and realized how fortunate I was to have my health, a roof over my head, and enough food to fill, or overfill, my stomach. I moved from room to room staring at the walls and started thinking about the money left for Mary, Bernard, and the man who lived in the apartment near Andy. I was confident the money had come from the sale of the stolen jewelry and the Baby Jesus. Mary was certain her note said the money was from Tiffany, and it wouldn't be a stretch to conclude Bernard's had as well.

Regardless how kind and generous the gifts were, I kept coming back to how they may have been the result of thefts of jewelry, surfboards, and the statue. I prayed I was wrong, although doubted it after hearing Mary. Did the recipients of the anonymous cash know about the crimes I suspect had been committed to get the money? Probably not. Did the recipients need the cash? No doubt.

I grabbed a Diet Pepsi, moved to my comfortable chair in the living room and said out loud, "Mary, Bernard, Andy's neighbor." What do they have in common? Down on their luck was a given. But so were others on Folly, as there were everywhere. Two had received a note, and I'd bet Andy's neighbor got one, but hadn't mentioned it to Andy. Did the three know each other? I wasn't certain.

It struck me that there was something else each had in common other than being needy. Bernard, according to Cal, and by his own admission, because of his quick temper, was not welcomed at the area homeless shelters. Andy's neighbor told him he had too much pride to seek help from anyone. And, Mary had said she was ashamed of what had happened to her husband, so much that she wouldn't seek help. It was tenuous, but still a connection. The phone rang before I could give it more thought.

"I've figured it out," Charles said in response to, "Hello."

I sighed. "Anything in particular?"

"Baby Jesus thief. You home?"

I said yes; he said, "Be there in ten." The line went dead.

Nine minutes later, Charles pounded on the door.

He rushed past me into the house. He was rubbing his hands together. His coat was zipped up to his neck. He said, "Burrr," unzipped his coat, and threw it on the ottoman. He wore a navy sweatshirt with *UMaine* in white on the front.

"Get serious," he said and headed to the kitchen.

"I've figured it out."

I followed him as he got a Pepsi and plopped down at the kitchen table.

I sat opposite him. "Okay, who did it?"

He took a sip and leaned back in the chair. "Finley, surfer boy, Livers."

"The Finley who started the group to catch the thief?"

"Yep."

"The Finley who invited us to his house and asked us to help the surfers catch the thief?"

"The same one."

Over the years, we had become involved in murder investigations, which should have been none of our business. Through blind luck, a rare burst of skill, and stumbling on information the police were unaware of, we had solved some of the crimes. Much of our success had been because we had spent hours talking through the situation, bounced ideas, good, bad, and terrible, off each other, and somehow figured things out. It appeared we were heading down that path again.

"How do you figure?"

"Misdirection." He leaned forward. "Of everyone here, who looks the least guilty?"

"Preacher Burl, Chief LaMond, you, me, umm—"

"Finley," Charles said and nodded.

I wouldn't have put him far up on my list, but he would have been on it. "Go on."

"I was up half the night thinking about it. Finley started the surfer group so he'd look as innocent as the pope. To throw us off, he asked us to find the thief. What better way to keep us from suspecting him?"

"Preacher Burl asked me to find the person who stole the statue. By your logic, he would be as likely as Finley."

Charles shook his head. "See, that's where my all-night thinkin' paid off. Burl couldn't have done it because he was with us when the money was stolen from First Light."

"I wasn't saying Burl did it. I was pointing out that because someone asked us to help doesn't mean he's guilty."

He took another sip and tapped his forefinger on the table. "I'll give you that one. How about this: What do Bernard and Andy's neighbor have in common?" Before I could answer, he said, "Hard times," and leaned back in the chair. "Do you remember what Finley talked about two of the times we'd been with him?"

"He hoped the money collected by both Cal and Burl went to people who didn't benefit from the regular groups serving the homeless."

Charles held out both hands. "You do pay attention. And then money shows up at Bernard's sleeping bag and the neighbor's door. Chris, it's Finley. I know it."

I wasn't ready to concede he was right and remembered other surfers had said the same thing about the underserved homeless, but knew the next thing I was going to tell him would have him pulling a muscle trying to pat himself on the back and then reaching for the phone to call the police. I slipped the phone in my pocket and told him about Mary and the note. When I reached the part about her living next to Finley, I thought Charles was going to erupt.

"Wow," he said and jumped up and waved his hands in the air. "We got him. Let's call Cindy and Preacher Burl."

I motioned for him to sit. He returned to the chair and shouted another "Wow!"

"Charles, let's say you're—we're—right. What we don't have is the statue. Let's say Finley is the thief and if he doesn't still have it, he knows who he sold it to. What do you think the chances are he'll tell the police where it is?"

"None."

"I agree. I also think Finley is serious about wanting to help people who aren't served by the traditional agencies, people like Mary, Bernard, and the other guy." I took a deep breath and couldn't believe what I was going to say next.

"We need to talk to him."

Charles stared at me, scratched his head, and stared at me some more. "Chris, if I'd said it, you'd call me a bloomin' idiot, someone with a death wish, and a bunch of other things you college-educated logical thinkers could come up with. Have we died and you came back as me?"

"If Finley took the statue, the only chance we have of getting it back is to talk to him. It's not much of a chance, but it's a chance. And, I don't have a death wish. We could call him and see if he would meet us at a public place. We could tell him we found something about the thefts and wanted him to know before we called the police. I'll offer to buy him supper."

Charles looked at his Pepsi, and at me, and shrugged. "What're you waiting for?"

Finley answered on the second ring. Music blared in the background, and I had to yell for him to hear who it was. The music stopped, and I lowered my voice and made the pitch to share information about the thefts and supper. He hesitated but agreed.

CHAPTER 22

Finley had chosen to meet us at Planet Follywood at six-thirty, and as sure as clockwork—Charles's clockwork—he and I arrived at six. There was one vacant table, the same table Mayor Newman and I had shared a few days earlier. From the jukebox, Bob Marley's distinct voice bopped through "Get Up, Stand Up."

Charles looked at the entry and at me. "Before you ask if I'm going to say, 'Hey, Finley, steal any Baby Jesus statues lately?' what's your plan to get a confession?"

"I've got an idea and still have thirty minutes to figure the rest of it out. I hope he's as concerned about the underdog as I think he is."

"Hi, guys."

I looked up, and Camille was at the table and setting a glass of Cabernet in front of me and a Bud Light beside Charles. She said, "Anything to eat?" I told her we were waiting for someone, and she said to wave when we needed her.

I took a sip and stared at the Christmas tree beside the jukebox. The lights were much brighter and more festive than I felt. Did my plan make sense? Earlier it sounded like a good idea to talk to Finley, but now I was beginning to agree with Charles. I was a bloomin' idiot.

Charles was facing the door and cleared his throat as he nodded toward it. I looked over my shoulder and saw Finley in the entry. He looked around and spotted us. He took a step back, hesitated, appeared to take a deep breath and headed our way. I hoped we didn't look as nervous as he did.

I moved around to Charles's side of the table and pointed to the seat where I had been sitting. Finley gave a slight nod and took the seat.

Charles said, "Bad day for surfin'."

He was trying to put Finley at ease since to Charles every day was a bad day for surfing.

"You bet."

Camille was back at the table and asked if Finley wanted anything. He looked at what we were drinking and said water.

I glanced at Charles who for once was keeping his mouth shut. The ball was in my court. I turned to Finley. "We appreciate how much you've done with your surfer group to make sure nobody takes anything from the Nativity, and the collection you took at the surf shop will help the needy. It took a lot of work to organize the group."

Finley said, "Too bad it didn't work." He looked at the Christmas tree and back at me. "You said you had something about the stealing."

The Beach Boys version of "Little St. Nick" blasted from the jukebox, the savory smell of hamburgers filled the air, and it was my turn to attempt to save the spirit of Christmas for Preacher Burl, First Light Church, and all who had been hurt by the disappearance of the iconic statue.

"Yes, and I think you'll find it interesting. There might still be time to get it back," I said and received a stare from Charles and a shrug from Finley.

"Charles and I decided the only thing we were interested in was finding the statue. We don't care about the

jewelry or the surfboards. Insurance will take care of it."
Charles looked at me like *we did?* "Remember the money
someone left Andy's neighbor?"

Finley said, "Sure."

"I've learned someone had left money for Bernard, a
homeless man, and for your friend Mary. They don't know
who gave it to them. We're pretty sure we do. Have you
heard about it?"

"Umm, don't think so."

Wouldn't yes or a no have been the right answer? I
began the story, which sounded much better earlier than it
did now.

"Do you know the guy who lives across the street and
up a house from you? It's the brick one." I asked, and crossed
my fingers the answer was no.

"I don't recall ever seeing anyone there. Don't know
who it is."

"That makes sense," I said. "Jimmy Russell's a
friend, about my age. He travels with his job; gone weeks at
a time. Because he's gone so much, he has a security system
that monitors the inside of his house for movement, and he
has cameras inside and outside that keep watch on his
property."

Thank you, Cindy, for giving me the idea about
cameras from you talking the other day about someone
capturing the video of someone leaving the porch after
stealing the ink cartridges.

Camille returned with Finley's water. Charles and I
ordered burgers and fries, and Finley said, "The same."

I took a deep breath and continued, "I don't
understand how it works, but through some high-tech
gadget, he can monitor the system from anywhere through
his telephone. He said it records a couple of weeks of data,
and he also can see what the cameras see in real time."

Finley said, "I've heard of that stuff."

Charles looked like he was afraid to break into my

story since he didn't know where it was going. All I hoped was he didn't ask who Jimmy Russell was. I didn't know where I was going either, but I continued talking slower than I was thinking.

"Jimmy's been in Oklahoma all month working with a company installing a new computer system. He thought he'd be home for Christmas, but it looks like he'll be stuck there until January."

"That's too bad," Charles added. "I'll miss seeing him at Cal's."

Charles couldn't bear for me to have a friend we didn't share, even an imaginary one.

"Me too," I said to Charles, and returned to Finley. "Jimmy doesn't have family here so it won't be too bad. Anyway, it's way more than you probably want to know. The important thing is he called this morning, and after he told me he wouldn't be here Christmas, he asked what had been going on since he'd been away. I told him about the missing statue, the theft of jewelry and surfboards, and the mysterious cash people had been receiving."

Our food arrived, and another reggae song reverberated off the walls. We each took a bite—Charles and Finley, because they were hungry, and me to stall until I figured out what to say.

I took another breath and said, "Jimmy asked a strange question. He asked if the lady with the two kids who got the money was staying in the house across from his. He said he'd seen a woman with two children coming and going. He knew the house was a rental and was surprised to see three people since there wasn't a car in the drive. Jimmy's a *live and let live* person, and said he didn't care how or why she was there. I told him it was Mary."

Finley fiddled with his fries and stared at his plate. I took a bite of the burger, and impatient Charles said, "So?"

"Here's the interesting part, Finley. Jimmy called me back later and said because of our conversation, he'd reviewed the video that had been recorded and a few days ago one of the cameras caught someone looking like he was sneaking up to Mary's back door and then running back in the direction he'd come from. Jimmy said it seemed strange and wondered if it had anything to do with her getting the money." I paused to let it sink in. "I asked him to describe the person. He said the guy was dressed in black, about your height Finley, and his head was covered with a hoodie."

Finley said, "Are you—"

I waved for him to stop, and continued, "Jimmy said the guy was running back to the house where he had come from. Funny thing Finley, it was your house."

It was my imagination, but it seemed like the world had stopped. If music was playing, I didn't hear it. If people in the crowded room were talking, I couldn't hear them. Was my bluff going to work, or was he going to laugh at me and walk out?

He looked at his burger. Charles was silent, for a change. And, my heart thumped like a bass drum.

Finley picked up his fork and pointed it at me, and started to speak. He shook his head and returned the fork to the table. Silence was deafening until he said, "Mr. Landrum, I'm not a thief. I didn't steal anything. Your friend didn't see me. He couldn't have because I never went over there."

Crap, I thought. I had begun to believe my story. I glanced at Charles, and he looked as dejected as I felt.

Then Finley said, "What if I can get the statue back?"

Charles leaned forward. "How?"

"I don't know for certain if I can, but I think I know what happened to it."

"How?" I asked.

"Are you going to turn me in to the cops?"

"Don't plan to," Charles said.

That's the truth since we didn't know any reason to—yet.

160

"Dude said I can trust you, so I'm taking him at his word. I honest to God didn't know anything about it until the other day. When I started the surfer group, I hoped we could catch the thief and get the Baby Jesus back to the church. I didn't know about the money for Andy's neighbor." He stopped and caught Camille's attention. "Think I need a beer." He turned back to Charles and me, lowered his voice, and said, "I saw the person take money to Mary's."

Charles interrupted, "Who?"

Finley shook his head. "Sorry, Mr. Fowler. I'm not going to tell you."

I didn't want him to stop talking. "That's okay, Finley. You said you might be able to get the statue back."

"Yeah, maybe. I didn't put two and two together until I saw, umm, the person leaving the money for Mary. I know he, or she, didn't have any to give so he, or she, had to steal the stuff. The next time I saw the person I said what I had seen and asked if he, or she, stole the Baby Jesus, the jewelry, and the other things. Then he or, never mind, I'll say he to make it easier to talk about. It don't mean it was a *he*."

I nodded. "Go on."

"He told me, yes, but if I went to the cops he'd deny it, and there wouldn't be any proof. I asked why he did it, and he said he was tired of seeing so many people in hapless straights who weren't being helped by poverty agencies. He knew agencies were doing a good job, but there were folks who for one reason or another had fallen through the cracks, the invisible ones I had talked about before."

"I remember you mentioning it in one of the meetings," I said, wanting to make him comfortable and to continue talking.

"The person who took the stuff told me he'd heard the statue was valuable. He didn't know why and confessed if he had known the story behind it, he wouldn't have taken it. He said he knew someone in Charleston who would buy it for a bunch of money, something about the person having a buyer he thought would want it. The other stuff was taken to hock. He was going to give every cent of what he got to the people he felt were in greatest need. He said he left bunches of money for people we haven't even heard about." He hesitated, glanced at Charles, and back at me. "Did you know Bernard's a war hero, has all sorts of medals, but came home from Afghanistan with a bad head injury. It knocked some of his memory out and left him with a bad temper."

I had known something was wrong but didn't know why, and it possibly explained his confusing Tiffany for Tabatha. I said, "VA would help him."

Finley shook his head. "Yeah, if he'd let them. He won't. Don't know why, but he's walked away from several VA facilities. They can't make him stay."

I said, "That's too bad."

Charles said, "So how can you get the statue back?"

"You sure you're not going to the cops?"

In twenty-four hours First Light will be holding its Christmas Eve service. Getting the statue back was more important than anything else. The thefts from the porches were another matter, one I'd deal with later.

I nodded. "Yes."

"How can you get it back?" Charles repeated.

"I'm not certain I can. A person in Charleston bought the statue, paid good money for it. He told the person who took it that the man he was going to sell it to lived out of state and was going to come to Charleston to get it in a few days. I don't know what a few days meant. He might already have it, and it's long gone."

"So it could still be in Charleston," I said. "If it is, how will you get it?"

He took a sip of beer. "I don't know."

Charles said, "Let us help."

Finley looked at the bottle and at Charles. "No. This is on me."

I didn't want to push more than we already had. "Okay, if you need anything or think of anything we can do, call me."

"Sure."

He slid his chair back, stood, and scurried out of the restaurant.

Bruce Springsteen's version of "Santa Claus is Coming to Town" filled the room and I wondered if the Baby Jesus would be coming back to town.

CHAPTER 23

Charles and I stayed in Planet Follywood and debated what to do. We could tell Cindy what we knew, or thought we knew, but we had no proof and if the police got involved, Finley's chances of getting the statue would vanish. Besides, the chief may think the three people we knew who'd received cash had been involved and could get them in trouble. I wasn't going to let that happen. Charles suggested we could follow Finley, and if he got in a tight spot, we could help. The more we talked about that idea, the worse it sounded.

We speculated who the thief was, concluded it was one of the surfers, but that only narrowed it down to a dozen or more people, and those were the people we had seen or met at the meetings. There could be others we didn't know. So, that was little help. It could also be Finley, and he made up the story to get off the hook. As much as it went against Charles's grain, we decided the best course of action was to wait and hope Finley had told us the truth and was able to get the statue back. The only good news was when Camilla told us the temperature tomorrow was going to be warm. It may not have made the children who had hoped for a rare dusting of snow happy, but it was great news for Preacher

Burl who could hold his Christmas Eve service on the beach.

I had a hard time going to sleep. I played Finley's words over in my head. I couldn't remember everything that was said when I was around the surfers and at the meetings, but I kept thinking there were others who were concerned about people who had fallen through the social services safety net. Ryan and Truman rented the second floor from Finley so he had more contact with them than the others. Hadn't Teddye said something? I wondered why Finley had been so concerned about saying he or she. Most people would have said he, regardless of gender. Did it mean anything or was I grasping for answers?

I didn't know about the temperature, but the weather forecasters were right about Christmas Eve being cloudless. Beams of sunshine streamed through the bedroom window, and I realized I had slept a couple of hours later than usual. I also realized I was hungry, so I walked to Bert's, received a cheerful "Merry Christmas Eve," from Eric, grabbed a cup of coffee, and remembered how good the mini donuts looked that Mary's children ate. I bought a pack, and walked to the Tides Hotel where I could sit in a comfortable chair in the lobby and look at the ocean.

"Come to help us?" I turned and saw Jamie, a longtime employee of the hotel and leader of the Folly Beach Bluegrass Society. He was holding a large, clear plastic bag stuffed with ropes.

"Going to hang someone?" I said.

"Not a bad idea, but not on Christmas Eve. We're putting up a tent on the other side of the pier."

The hotel rented tents for special events although I couldn't imagine a wedding reception or any other kind of event today. "What's the event?"

"We heard Preacher Burl was having Christmas Eve service on the beach, and a few of us decided it may get cold and windy, so we pitched in and rented a tent. The hotel helped. We're putting it up now. It's terrible about the Baby

Jesus; thought it would be something we could do."

I told him I'd stop by after finishing my healthy breakfast.

Jamie looked at the donuts and the powdered sugar on my shirt. "No hurry. At your age, you couldn't be much help." He chuckled and walked away.

I saw little humor in his comment, but he was right. I continued eating the donuts and wondering when, or if, I would be hearing from Finley. It wasn't ten o'clock, but I was as impatient as Charles.

It turned out to be a beautiful Christmas Eve. Reflections of the sun sparkled off the calm ocean; the temperature was in the low-sixties and several people were walking on the beach and around town in shirtsleeves. I decided not to go home because if I did, I would stare at the phone and worry about when or if Finley would call. I dropped by a couple of shops and talked with the owners about the weather, and how early they would be closing. At each store, I had to answer if there was anything new about the statue. As much as I wanted to, it was impossible to get it off my mind. I grabbed a quick lunch at the Crab Shack, walked to the small Folly River Park overlooking the river and admired the large, real, Christmas tree covered in colorful lights and ornaments as it watched over the park. It was surrounded by other decorations, which brought joy to young and old. I stared at the river, and headed back to the Folly pier. At the intersection that led to Pewter Hardware and First Light's Nativity, I saw Samuel and Jason sitting on the incline leading to the edge of the park. Their bikes were on the ground beside them, and they stared at the display.

I shook my head and walked the half block to the teens. "Merry Christmas Eve, guys."

They had watched me walking toward them, stood, and wiped the dust off the back of their jeans. Jason looked across the street at the Nativity and at me. "What's merry about it, Mr. Landrum? We failed."

"You didn't fail. You've done everything you could. You found the ink cartridges. You've asked students about the statue. And Jason, to tell you the truth, even though you got me in trouble with your mom, I'm impressed how hard you've worked to help. No, you didn't fail."

Samuel looked at Jason to see if he was going to say anything. He didn't, and Samuel turned to me. "All we wanted was to find Baby Jesus, and all we found was some stupid ink." He pointed to the manger. "Jason's right, we failed."

"You didn't find the statue, but Christmas is more than a carved piece of wood. It's a time to celebrate the birth of the real Jesus. That will happen if the statue is over there or not. It's time to think about all the good in our lives. Jason, you have a great mom," I smiled, "and she has a great son. And Samuel, I don't know your dad as well as I do Jason's mom, but from everything I know, he's a wonderful dad. Think how lucky you are."

"I guess you're sort of right," Samuel said. "But we also know how much the statue means to people."

I looked at the distraught teen. "Many of them will be at church tonight. Why don't you come and look at all the good we have and celebrate instead of the bad stuff that's happened?"

Jason looked at the ground and glanced at Samuel before saying, "Don't worry, Mr. Landrum, we'll be there. Mom'll kill me if I'm not."

Samuel giggled. "Dad will too."

"What's so funny?"

Samuel said, "Dad and Jason's mom are sort of coming to church together."

It surprised me more than him giggling. "A date?"

Samuel patted Jason's arm. "Sort of. He said they are doing it because we're friends. He said they might as well be friends too."

Jason laughed. "Ain't it a crock?"

I looked at Jason. "I think it's nice."

Jason said. "I think it's weird."

To my knowledge, Amber hadn't dated since we'd broken up. To be honest, I didn't know what to think other than I was happy for them and while I hadn't thought of them together, I had a good feeling about it.

"See you tonight," I said as they mounted their bikes and peddled away. If the rest of the teenagers growing up on Folly were half as good as those two, the island's future was in good hands.

I continued to the pier and walked about halfway to the end and looked at the large, white tent at the spot on the beach where First Light met in nice weather. Jamie and a couple of his helpers were carrying folding chairs to the tent from a trailer at the beach access point. I was touched by how the island's residents, regardless of social status, wealth, beliefs, and differences came together to help each other in the time of need. I had seen this level of community support numerous times. I also thought of the misery, demons, and helplessness Bernard must be going through, and how Mary must be having mixed thoughts about how wonderful it was to have her two girls with her, but feeling the weight of such a bleak outlook for their future. I didn't know Andy's neighbor or the other people who had received money but hoped the anonymous gifts had brought cheer and hope.

I had never been a fan of telephones, but I couldn't recall wanting one to ring more than I did at this moment. It was three o'clock, four short hours until First Light's service, and nothing from Finley. Thirty more minutes had passed before I heard the much-awaited ring. The screen showed a number I didn't recognize. I would normally have let it go to voicemail, but not today.

"Mr. Landrum, this is Finley."

I had long championed a more civil and hospitable way of answering the phone. I abandoned my crusade and blurted, "Did you get it?"

There was silence on the other end; I wondered if he had heard my question. I caught myself holding my breath.

"No."

I lowered myself on one of the benches that dotted the pier. "What happened?"

"I tried," Finley said, sounding as depressed as I felt. "Honest, I tried."

"I'm sure you did. What happened?"

"I went to the place that bought it and told the guy I was a friend of, umm, the person who took it. I made up a story and told him my friend had taken it by mistake, and the statue meant a lot to the owner. I told him I'd buy it back." Finley hesitated. "I didn't know where I'd get the money. I figured you and Charles, and maybe the preacher could help. The slimy son of a ... the guy said he'd seen on television where the statue had been stolen, and he didn't think I was telling the truth. He said two old guys had come around asking about buying a wood carved statue from Germany. He said he didn't know how stupid I thought he was, or how stupid the old guys thought he was, but he knew my story was a bunch of sh—umm, crap."

"What did you say?"

"I didn't know what to say, Mr. Landrum. I didn't confess to lying to him but told him how important the Baby Jesus was to the church and even to people who don't go to church over here. I figured he wouldn't call the police after what I knew about him, but I was afraid he was going to throw me out on my ass. Anyway, he calmed down a little and said he was sorry about the missing Jesus, and he was busy and couldn't talk any longer. Busy, huh? I was the only person in his store. I didn't argue with him." Finley sighed. "What else could I have done, Mr. Landrum?"

I assured him there wasn't anything and thanked him for trying.

He said, "Sorry," and hung up.

"Me too," I said to silent air.

CHAPTER 24

The sun had set an hour and a half before I walked to the beach, head down, and feeling like I'd failed Preacher Burl. Three, duel-headed halogen lights on telescoping stands illuminated the inside of the tent. The heavy-duty work lights were in the rear of the tent, and their power cords snaked across the sand to an electric box under the pier. Solar-powered pathway lights were placed in the sand every six feet to light the way to the service.

Jamie leaned against a post at the beach access point. He looked exhausted but was smiling.

"Where'd all this come from?"

He shrugged. "Called in favors. Got everything donated. It'd take a cold-hearted person to turn down helping a church on Christmas Eve. Besides, I know a thing or two about the builder I got most of the stuff from." He chuckled. "He'd rather I don't share what I know."

Charles had been standing by the tent and came over to Jamie and me. It was a half hour before the service was to begin so we stayed with Jamie as a few other early birds arrived. Charles stared at me. I knew what he wanted, but I wasn't ready to tell him. Jamie said he had a volunteer crew from the hotel who would take everything down after the service, and he'd better check in and make sure they would be around when he needed them. I thanked him for his effort; he grinned and said he didn't do it for me, but would accept thanks anyway.

Charles leaned closer. "Okay, I was trying not to be my nosy, nervous, impatient self, being it's Christmas Eve, but we've been standing here ten minutes."

"Yes," I said.

"And I haven't pestered you about what you learned from Finley. And, you've not thought it was important enough to say anything about it."

I looked at the tent and at Charles. "Suppose I didn't want to say it. Finley talked to the man who bought the statue and offered to buy it back. He wouldn't sell. He told Finley two *old* men had been to see him, but he had known about the thefts and figured the *old* guys were trying to trick him."

"So it was one of the antique dealers. Damn."

"I heard that." We turned, and Burl was standing five feet away.

Charles took off his Tilley and bowed in Burl's direction. "Sorry, Preacher."

Burl waved the apology off. "What pray tell caused such an utterance, Brother Charles?"

Charles turned to me, and I realized Burl didn't know about Finley. This wasn't the time to get into it.

"Charles was expressing disappointment that Baby Jesus hadn't been found."

Burl frowned. "I echo his sentiment, but perhaps would have chosen another expression. As disheartening as it is, I am focusing on the positive and refuse to let whatever happened to the icon ruin such a glorious night on the eve of celebrating our Savior's birth."

Dude and Pluto were next to join us. In addition to Pluto's rhinestone covered collar and leash, he wore a red and white striped sweater. Dude wore typical Dude. Burl smiled and suggested we move to the "magnificent sanctuary provided by the good folks of Folly." We took it to mean the tent and followed him. Lottie was seated near the front as we stepped under the tent. A steady cool breeze had been coming off the ocean all afternoon, and Jamie had lowered all the sides except the back flap. Before Burl moved inside, he slipped his robe over his jacket. He moved to the portable lectern and placed his Bible and a folder on top of it.

Next to arrive was Dude's snarky employee Stephon, followed closely by Teddye, Deb, Truman, and Finley. The group looked around and mumbled something I couldn't hear. Burl was quick to reach them and gave his best pastoral smile, told them he was thrilled they were here and told them to take seats of their choice.

Others arrived in clumps. Members of other congregations appeared, I assumed to show support for First Light. Another of the surfers, Todd, arrived by himself and quickly attached himself to Truman and Finley. Samuel's dad, Jacob looked around the corner of the tent and stepped inside; Amber was at his side. I was glad their sons had told me about them coming together. They looked around and headed to the back row, left two seats vacant, and sat in the next two.

Bernard arrived next and had on his new jacket and wore a look on his face that looked like a combination of fear and confusion. I rushed to him and said, "It's good to see you."

"Thank you, sir. I almost chickened out. I'm not comfortable in crowds."

I wanted to ask if the name on the note could have been Tiffany, but figured now it didn't matter. I said, "You'll be fine. You can sit with Charles and me if you'd like."

"I might." He nodded and walked over to Finley and said something.

I spoke to George and Shelesa Brew, a couple I recognized from my gallery and knew were regulars at the Catholic Church, and they introduced me to their friends Jim and Dianne Stevens. I told them how much Preacher Burl appreciated their support, and excused myself. I then walked over to Jacob and Amber and said I was glad to see them together. Jacob blinked twice, looked at Amber, and said, "Thank you, Chris. Amber and I've shared a few meals. She's quite a lady." He patted her arm.

I smiled. "Yes she is. Where're the boys?"

Amber looked around. "They're on their way. It's irritating, they're getting more unreliable all the time." She looked at me like it was my fault and then looked at her watch.

"They're teenagers," Jacob said. "Doubt we were any better when we were their age."

Amber grinned. "You're right."

Burl tapped on the lectern—pulpit—with his Bible. "Please take thy comfortable seats provided by the good and generous folks at the Tides."

The harsh halogen lights gave Burl a deer in the headlights look. He blinked a few times before his eyes adjusted to the unflattering lighting. Even with that distraction, his smile was infectious. He began with his traditional *silence thy portable communication devices* opening and looked toward the back of the room, paused, and waved for someone to come in.

I turned and saw Mary and her girls step in the tent, and at the preacher's urging, walked to four empty seats in the next to last row. Mary was wearing her new coat and gingerly stepped through the sand in shiny shoes, which looked to be as new as the coat. She held her shoulders back, her head held high, and motioned for the girls to take the seats beside her.

Burl smiled at the latecomers. "Welcome ladies. Welcome."

At the same time, I caught someone else entering from the back. I was surprised to see Karen looking around the tent. She had called yesterday and said she didn't think she'd make it. A man was sitting beside me, but there was an empty chair on the other side of him. I asked if he would mind moving one chair over. He noticed Karen, grinned at me, and scooted to the next seat.

She took the empty seat and leaned close and whispered, "Sorry for being late. The dead don't keep good track of time."

"Thanks for coming," was all I said before Burl asked us to stand and sing "O Come, All Ye Faithful."

We stood, tried to sing, and if nothing else, sounded spirited. After our enthusiastic, although off-key effort, Burl thanked us for attending, and gave a special thanks to everyone who had helped make the service possible. He opened his folder and glanced down before continuing.

I looked around and wondered if the thief was here, and then focused on Burl.

"Tonight's not about First Light, not about me, it's about everyone. It's about faith. It's about hope. It's not about the past and whatever has been negatively tugging at our minds and bodies. We're gathered to look to the future. I know several of you are members of other congregations on our incredible island. You've been part of the dedicated group who have watched over the Nativity day and night, and have shared with me you are in attendance to show solidarity. Some of you are part of the caring surfer community who has been standing sentry at the symbol of our Lord's birth." He smiled. "Some of you do not attend church on a regular basis but feel compelled to visit a place of worship at Christmas. I say to each of you, regardless of your reason, welcome. I love you, God loves you." He squinted at the bright lights as he looked out at the assembled group. "Please stand and let's join together and blend our melodious voices into singing "The First Noel."

Once again, the group made a valiant effort to not sound like a flock of seagulls fighting over a fish. Perhaps I was in the Christmas spirit, because the singing sounded pleasant.

We finished singing, *Born is the King of Israel!* and Preacher Burl motioned for us to be seated. We did and waited for him to continue. Instead, he stared at the back of the tent, his mouth opened, but no words came out. I turned to see what he was looking at.

Samuel and Jason were at the entry. Their coats were zipped up to their neck, each had a huge smile, and they were holding a dark green blanket wrapped around something. By now, a few of the others had turned to see what had stopped the service. Jason pushed the top of the blanket to the side, and I could see a tiny head peeking through—the head of a hand carved, statue of the Baby Jesus.

Jason and Samuel's smiles were so captivating I barely heard Preacher Burl scream, "Halleluiah!" The next thing I saw was Amber and Jacob rushing to their sons. They beat Burl by a half step.

Samuel cradled the Baby Jesus in his arms and held them out to the preacher. Burl took the statue, which was still wrapped in the blanket and held it close to his chest. He whispered something to the boys; Jason said something, and Burl walked to the front of the church. The boys followed as did Amber and Jacob. There were low mumblings from some of the flock, but most of us stood and stared at the group assembled at the lectern. Burl said something to Amber and Jacob, and they moved behind their sons. The boys glanced at Burl and down at the sand. Burl motioned for us to be seated.

"Brothers and sisters," he said, his voice stronger than ever. "We have witnessed a miracle, the type of miracle that can only come from God. Please join me in silent prayer."

The only sounds that could be heard were a couple of vehicles on Arctic Avenue and the faint sounds of live music from a nearby bar.

Burl broke the silence. "Brothers Jason and Samuel have agreed to share how they came upon the miracle I am now holding to my bosom." He looked at Jason. Jason turned to Samuel, who gave him a dirty look and said, "Thanks a lot."

Samuel started to speak to the group, hesitated and moved behind the lectern. He was five inches taller than the preacher and visible to everyone.

"Umm, hi folks." He hesitated and glanced at Burl and back at the group before him. "Hi, flock people. Preacher Burl asked us to tell how we found Baby Jesus. Well, some of you know Jason and I have been looking for the missing baby since we heard it'd been snatched." He smiled. "My friend here, Jason, got in trouble from his mom for us nosing around the island—sorry about that, Mrs. Lewis. Anyway, Mr. Landrum told us we better stop nosing around in people's trash, so we sort of did stop. We almost gave up on finding it, and we were on our way over here a little while ago when Jason said we ought to ride by the Nativity one more time. He said you surfers and church people who have been watching it would have stopped and headed to church. Isn't that right, Jason?"

Jason nodded and motioned for Samuel to continue.

"Well, we sort of rode by and almost didn't see it. The Baby Jesus, the man from the Methodist Church lent the Nativity, was lying in back in the hay. And holy moly, there was another baby's head sticking out of the manger. I was so excited I nearly ran my bike into a pole before I could stop." He paused and looked at me. "I know, I know, Mr. Landrum. The bad guy could still be there and get us in trouble. We looked around all cautious like and didn't see anyone so we thought it was safe. Jason said we shouldn't be carrying a baby around on our bikes, even if it was made out of wood, so I rushed home and got this blanket while Jason stayed with Jesus." He lifted the corner of the blanket up so everyone could see it. "We came here, and that's the entire story."

Jason leaned toward Samuel and said, "The note."

Samuel reached into his jacket pocket and pulled out a small slip of paper. "Oh yeah, stuck under the baby's head was this." He held the paper in the air. "It says, *Merry Christmas.* He turned the note over and looked at the back of it and turned it back to the front. "That's all it says. Don't it beat all?"

I couldn't have said it better; differently, but not better. I looked around and saw tears in Mary's eyes, and Amber and Jacob were beaming. Preacher Burl wiped a tear from his eye, put his arms around the boys, and then took the statue and its blanket from Jason and placed it on the lectern.

Charles leaned over and said, "I suppose sometime in my many years on this earth, I have been happier, but for the life of me, I can't remember when."

Preacher Burl took a couple of deep breaths, looked at the carved statue, and motioned for us to stand. "How about singing "Away in a Manger"?" He had lost track of where he was in the service, but I doubted anyone cared. I could feel the excitement in the tent as we stood and began:

> *Away in a manger, no crib for a bed,*
> *The little Lord Jesus lay down His sweet head.*
> *The stars in the bright sky looked down where He lay,*
> *The little Lord Jesus asleep on the hay.*

Some of us got several of the words right; none of us appeared to care. Pure joy filled the spaces unoccupied by the correct lyrics.

CHAPTER 25

I spent Christmas morning walking around town and enjoying the warm weather. I grabbed coffee from Bert's, received a hardy "Merry Christmas," from Eric, who was way too cheery for someone who had to work Christmas Day. I chuckled at his words, and the red Christmas hat that adorned his well-maned head. I walked to the Folly River Park, looked out at the one small boat meandering downstream, and walked over to the Nativity, the site of the crime, which had nearly stolen the spirit of Christmas from the community. No surfers or church members were looking over the empty manger. The town was silent, not quite *not a creature was stirring* quiet, but close. I smiled as I thought about the look on Preacher Burl's face when Jason and Samuel entered with the statue.

I didn't know who had taken the icon, nor who had stolen the packages or the surfboards off the porches, but I had a strong suspicion. What was I going to do about it? I couldn't prove it. If I was right, the thefts were to get money to help people who needed it the most. Admirable, but stealing was stealing. So, why was I so conflicted about what to do? Maybe it was because I had seen the look in Mary's eyes when she could do something good for her children.

Perhaps it was because I saw the glimmer of hope in Bernard's confused and distressed mind when he could buy groceries and know someone did care about him. I imagined the neighbor who had received the early, and unexpected Christmas gift as he went through a tough time, had also felt gratitude and the strength to get back on his feet. Maybe…maybe I don't know. I did know it was time to get to Cal's party.

The smell of fries met me at the door, the sounds of laughter filled the room, and the festive colors of Christmas lights twinkled from most every surface as well as from the multiple Christmas trees. It was early afternoon, and Cal's Country Christmas Celebration was in full swing. The jukebox, normally full of country classics, had been stuffed with Christmas tunes, and as unbelievable as it may have been to regulars, some of the songs weren't being performed by country artists who were either crooning for their Master or spending eternity in a much warmer climate. Harry Connick, Jr.'s version of "Jingle Bells" could be heard between bursts of laughter. Cal's Christmas day celebration had grown to be one of Folly's most popular events, especially for those who didn't have families to spend the holiday with.

Charles was the first to notice me. I almost didn't recognize him since he had abandoned his college mascot sweatshirts and had on a bright red one with a giant Santa's head on the front.

"About time you got here," he said.

"Merry Christmas to you, too."

He put his arm around my shoulders. "I'll let you sugarcoat being late. It's Christmas." He looked behind me. "Where's Karen? She told me last night she'd be coming with you."

"She called this morning. Another death."

Our conversation was interrupted when Cal tapped on a vintage, baseball-sized silver microphone in the center of the tiny stage. "Let this old cowboy interrupt your celebrating for a minute."

Most of the gathered group stopped talking and turned to the stage. One group kept talking and Cal, tapped on the mike. "To paraphrase a preacher I know, please silence thy big mouths."

That got everyone's attention. Cal grinned, the twinkling lights on the crown of his Stetson matched the smile on his face. "I wanted to thank ya'll. This is the fourth year I've had this shindig, and this is the best by a Texas mile. Now some of you have asked if I'd sing a few Christmas ditties so who am I to turn down such nice requests?"

It wouldn't have taken many requests to tempt him. He took his guitar out of the case, strummed a couple of chords, and said, "I'll start with a song my good buddy, Gene Autry, made famous a few years back. Some of you may know it. It's called "Rudolph the Red-Nosed Reindeer."

Cal's *few years back* happened to be before I was born, and from the number of people in the room who started singing along with him, "Some of you may know it," was a Texas-sized understatement. Charles said he was going to spread some Christmas cheer and headed toward the bar. I looked around the room and saw many of the people who had been at the Christmas Eve service. I was surprised to see Dude's employee, Stephon. He was standing at the bar, sipping a beer, and frowning, but at least he was here. I recognized a few of the surfers I had met in the last two weeks. Teddye and Finley were huddled in discussion at one of the tables, and Roscoe, Todd, Slick Surfin' Sal, and Ryan were at the adjoining table watching Cal as he finished singing and placed his guitar back in the case.

Cal said, "Be back a little later with a couple of more of my favorite Christmas songs." He pointed his finger at me, stepped off the stage, and headed my way.

I said, "Merry Christmas. Looks like a full house."

He gave me an awkward hug and said, "Ain't it great news about the Baby Jesus coming home?"

I said it was as he reached in his back pocket. He said, "Was wondering when you'd get here. Got something for you." He pulled out a light-gray envelope and handed it to me. It was addressed *Chris and Charles*.

I shrugged and took it from him. "Where'd it come from?"

"Found it under the door when I opened up this morning."

I looked for Charles. He was talking to Mel Evans and his significant other Caldwell. I caught his eye and he said something to Mel and came over to Cal and me. I showed him the envelope and yanked it back when he tried to grab it out of my hand. I opened it and pulled out a small sheet of paper the same color as the envelope. On the paper was a neatly printed note and I read it to Charles and Cal: *Sorry I stole the stuff. Didn't mean to hurt the city or the church. You see, I had to help my forgotten friends, the invisible ones. Couldn't think of any other way to do it. Please apologize to the preacher for me. He seems like a good person. Also, say I'm sorry to the police.*

Charles glanced at the paper. "Don't suppose it's signed?"

Cal removed his Stetson and pointed it at the note. "Holy horseradish. We've got a confession right here on Christmas Day."

Nat King Cole's version of "Frosty the Snowman" played from the jukebox and I stood silent and stared at the note.

As if on cue, Preacher Burl stepped in the door. I was surprised and pleased to see Lottie with him. They weren't walking hand in hand, but their body language said they weren't far from it. Burl saw Cal and headed our way.

"Merry Christmas, Brother Cal. Thanks for the invitation." He put his arm behind Lottie and nudged her closer to Cal. "You know my friend, Lottie, don't you?"

Cal tipped his Stetson to her. "I do. Welcome, Miss Lottie."

She smiled, thanked Cal for letting her come, and nodded to Charles and me.

"Preacher," Cal added, "I hear a herd of prayers was answered last night. Baby Jesus came home."

Burl said, "It was a Christmas miracle."

Cal looked at the note in my hand and turned to Burl. "Preacher there's something Chris wants to—"

Before Cal finished the sentence, Bernard stepped between Burl and Cal. "Please accept my apology for interrupting, Preacher Burl, sir. If I didn't say it now, I was afraid I never would."

Burl said, "That's okay. What's on your mind, Brother Bernard."

"Preacher, Mr. Landrum suggested I might be able to unload some, umm, burdens on your ears. He said you might be able to help. Do you think you could spend some time with me in the next few days? I'd appreciate it."

Burl glanced at Bernard and me. "I'd be honored, Brother Bernard. How about tomorrow morning? I'll be in our storefront sanctuary around nine."

"I'll be there, Preacher. Again, I apologize for interrupting. Merry Christmas."

Burl watched Bernard leave and turned to Cal. "You were saying."

Before Cal could mention the note, I said, "I wanted to say how wonderful I thought the service was last night."

Charles gave me a sideways glance and Cal opened his mouth and closed it. Burl thanked me and said the return of the statue made the night the best he's ever had.

Cal said, "Preacher walk up to the stage with me and help me sing a song."

"You know I'm a better preacher than a singer, but it's your party."

Cal and Burl headed to the stage and Charles said, "Why didn't you tell him about the note?"

I watched Cal and Burl on the stage and said, "It's Christmas."

Charles started to say something and I stopped him.

Cal, with his duet partner, sang, *Joy to the world! The Lord is Come.*

Mary and her children were the next to arrive. She smiled when she saw me with Charles. I waved her over. "Merry Christmas, Mary," I knelt down. "Merry Christmas, Jewel and Joanie."

The girls smiled and each held up a starfish. "Look what we got for Christmas," Jewel said.

"They're lovely."

The girls smiled; Mary beamed. And Cal and Burl finished with, *And wonders of his Love.*

"Ladies," Charles said, "How about let's go get something to drink? I bet that bartender can rustle up a Coke."

Mary hugged me and followed Charles, Jewel, and Joanie to the bar. I took the opportunity to look around for someone I hadn't seen yet. Still not seeing him, I walked to the group of surfers, nodded, and received lukewarm responses.

I put my hand on Finley's back. "Finley, could I borrow you a minute?"

He looked scared but said yes. I led him to the corner of the room where there were the fewest people.

I said, "Thank you for whatever you did to get the statue back."

"Mr. Landrum, I wish I could take credit. I didn't do anything more than what I told you. It was you who figured most of it out and made me try. All I can figure is the man who bought it felt guilty and brought it back."

"Maybe," I said. "Could the person who stole it in the first place have done something to get it back?"

"Yes."

"Like I told you before, all I cared about was the church getting the statue back, so whatever happened, I'm thankful."

He sighed. "Me too, Mr. Landrum."

I looked at him for a moment and asked, "Where's Truman? He was at church last night but I don't see him here."

Finley looked down at his shoes like he'd never seen them before. I waited, listened to a verse of "Frosty the Snowman" from the jukebox, and Finley said, "Umm, Don't know. I went upstairs to his room this morning to thank...umm...to see if he wanted to come with me." He hesitated again. "He was gone. His stuff was gone."

I wasn't surprised. "That's too bad. I wanted to wish him Merry Christmas."

Finley gave me a knowing glance. "I think he's having a good one, Mr. Landrum."

Cal tapped again on the mike to get our attention. I reached in my pocket and wadded up the note and turned to the stage.

"Ya'll join in," Cal said.

And the singing began:

> *Silent Night, Holy Night!*
> *All is calm, all is bright,*
> *'Round yon Virgin Mother and Child*
> *Holy Infant so tender and mild*
> *Sleep in heavenly peace,*
> *Sleep in heavenly peace.*

About the author:

Bill Noel is the author of the popular Folly Beach Mystery series that includes the titles *Folly*, *The Pier*, *Washout*, *The Edge*, *The Marsh*, *Ghosts*, *Missing*, *Final Cut*, *First Light,* and *Boneyard Beach*. He is a fine arts photographer and retired university administrator. Bill lives in Louisville, Kentucky, with his wife, Susan.

71097606R00107

Made in the USA
Columbia, SC
20 May 2017